THE CONFESSIONAL

A C.T. FERGUSON CRIME NOVELLA (#1)

TOM FOWLER

Do you like free books? You can get the prequel novella to the C.T. Ferguson mystery series for free. This is exclusive to my VIP readers. Just go here to get your book!

Editing by Chase Nottingham.

Cover design by 100Designs

 Created with Vellum

THERE COMES A POINT IN EVERYONE'S LIFE (well, almost everyone's) when the person realizes he or she isn't as smart as once thought. This realization is usually brought on by some cruel event to hammer the point home. The young man sitting on the other side of my desk just experienced this epiphany. And he didn't look happy about it.

"Let me make sure I have this right," I said. "You implicated yourself in a murder."

"Yes," he said with a nod.

"One you're telling me you didn't commit."

"Yes."

I sighed. When one operates a free detective business, one is beset with crackpots. My first two months on the job taught me this. "And you did this—why, exactly?" I said.

"For my blog," he said as if people confessed to murders they didn't commit all the time.

"For your blog."

"I'm doing a true crime podcast, too," he said, digging his hole deeper. My silence compelled him to keep talking. "A classmate suggested it."

"Your classmate is an imbecile," I said.

"Yanni's good with all the web stuff, even marketing. He does it for his dad's business."

"Someone named Yanni suggested your false admission?"

"Yes."

"You should ignore Yanni in the future. If you have a classmate named Kenny G, ignore him, too." I only knew of those two artists because my parents enjoyed them. My mother, well aware I disliked both, always played them when I visited. For a woman pushing sixty, her troll game was strong.

"Too late for that now," he said.

The young man's youthful, chubby face led me to guess his age as twenty. He was about five-ten, giving me four inches on him, and had a physique suggesting he updated his blog regularly. I looked at his coloration and features and—drawing on my thirty-nine months in China—concluded he was half-Chinese. When I judged his actions, I concluded he was all idiot.

"Sometimes, I wish I believed in regrets," I said. "You're going to have to give me something more than 'my classmate said so' or 'for my podcast.'"

"I run the *Murderphiles Blog*." He paused

there, waiting for me to react. I'd never heard of his site, so I shrugged. He sighed and continued. "It's going to be the podcast name, too. We've been getting a lot of good hits the past few months."

"I hope the Google Ads revenue can buy you a lawyer, then."

He waved a dismissive hand. "Look, I got inspired by *Serial*. A lot of murders happen in Baltimore." That was inescapably true. Season one of *Serial* focused on one such murder from almost twenty years ago. A lot more had taken place since. "The police don't tell us everything about them. The papers don't tell us everything. That's where we come in."

"Because victims' families love talking to low-rent Internet personalities?" I said.

"They want the truth," he said. "They want justice."

"Aren't their odds better in the legal system?"

"You're C.T. Ferguson. 'The P.I. who helps the little guy,' according to your ad. You run a free detective service." He frowned. "There's no way you're a big believer in the legal system."

He had me, even though I wished he'd omitted the dreadful tagline my father devised. Since no potential client ever put those pieces together before, I had had to give this fellow his props, at least in this narrow case. "I'd trust it over a guy with a blog," I said. "Especially when the guy with a blog does something colossally stupid."

The young man sighed. "What am I going to do? The police are after me to turn myself in."

"It's exactly what you should do."

"But I didn't kill anyone!"

"Then you shouldn't have inserted yourself into their case. The police are going to take an interest when you do."

"I figured the ploy would just get me some publicity and spur the investigation," he said. "I never thought it would get this far."

"But it has. You need to turn yourself in."

"Can I hire you?"

I laughed. Then I drank some water and laughed again. "Seriously?"

"You could find the real killer," he said.

"I don't work for morons," I said, and he frowned anew. "You got yourself into this mess because you wanted publicity for your budding media empire. It was stupid but mission accomplished. Now go deal with it. If you didn't do it, the police will figure it out."

"But I'll get arrested."

"Yes."

"And go to jail."

"What do you think happens when you arouse suspicion you may have committed a crime like murder?" I said.

The young man slumped in his chair. "You won't take this case?"

"Not a chance."

He got up and walked out. I shrugged, refilled my water bottle, and went online to check his precious blog.

* * *

AN HOUR LATER, I had read a bunch of articles on the blog. Other than my profound objection to the fake word "Murderphiles," I thought the site featured good content—minus the constant mentions of the upcoming podcast. I saw details news reports and police officers would exclude. All the information gained came from no special access or privilege. It was a good bit of reporting, especially for a blogger.

He turned out to be Ernest (Ernie) Chin. The blog resided on a paid site running WordPress, and for some reason, Ernie failed to remove himself from any of the Whois records. Every website lists contact information for the people responsible for registering and maintaining it. Those cataloged Ernie, his address, and phone number. I found him in about five seconds. Maybe I could help him by suggesting simple measures like anonymizing his info. Bloggers who go into deep details of grisly crimes shouldn't be broadcasting their personal information for the world to see. Not everyone knew about Whois records, but a killer would only need one friend who did.

Another hour later, I heard the Baltimore Police Department arrested Ernie Chin after he confessed to the murder of Dave Waugh. The media already found perverse delight in the fact that Ernie confessed and then tried to plead his innocence. Their delight must have stemmed from the fact he posted information they didn't. Old media will always hold a grudge against the new like the town crier despised a printed newssheet. I believed Ernie was innocent. More importantly, I believed he was stupid, and this would teach him the limits of driving traffic to his blog.

Later during the night, my cell phone rang. The caller showed as blocked. I try not to answer such calls, but the nature of my job compels me. "Hello?" I said.

An automated voice said, "This call originates from the Central Booking and Intake Facility in Baltimore, Maryland. Would you like to continue?"

Every instinct and scrap of common sense I had screamed to say no. Instead, I assented.

"C.T.?" said a voice I remembered from earlier.

"Why the hell are you calling me?" I said.

"I got arrested."

"Yes, Ernie. The whole city knows."

"You know my name."

"You really should check the box to anonymize your Whois records."

"Anyway," he said, "will you take my case now?"

I hung up on him.

He didn't call back. After another hour of Netflix, I went to bed.

* * *

THE NEXT MORNING, I ran through Fells Point, along the Baltimore Harbor, and back through the streets to my apartment. I liked the city at this hour. The downtown area bustled with cars and starched shirts, but Fells Point, several blocks removed, kept a lighter pace. Businesses were opening. Restaurants and bars started their daily prep. Aromas of coffee, bread, and seafood wafted through the brisk January air, urging me forward.

After a shower, I made breakfast in my smallish kitchen. It boasted enough counter space for me to work, but if I ever had a date serve as my lovely sous chef, the quarters would be tight. I chopped mushrooms and onions and shredded some fresh spinach, throwing it all in a pan to sauté. When everything had cooked nicely, I added the eggs. I put multigrain bread in the toaster while I tended the omelet, giving it a careful flip and adding a sprinkle of pepper jack cheese before I folded it. Somewhere, a French chef would cringe at my cheese choice (and my technique as well). I would console myself with a delicious omelet and the fact I wasn't French.

I was about halfway through my omelet when my phone rang. Another number I didn't recognize flashed across the screen. After a moment of consideration, my stomach emerged the victor, and I declined the call. Not one savory bite later, the same number called again. I answered this time.

"This is Liz Fleming with the Public Defender's office," said the lady on the other end. I liked her voice; it reminded me of a girl I dated for much of my sophomore year of college. My half-full gut told me her tone would be the only thing I liked about this conversation.

"I have a feeling I know why you're calling," I said.

"Let's hear it."

"You have a persistent cretin for a new client."

"I get a lot of cretins," Liz said. "Most of them are guilty. Few of them are persistent."

"Lucky you," I said, "but I can't help you."

"Can you come to my office?" Liz seemed undeterred by my rejection. Her persistence matched Ernie Chin's. I hoped she outstripped him in intelligence and common sense.

"When?"

"As soon as you can."

"I'm eating breakfast," I said. To emphasize the

point, I ate a bite of toast with my phone held to my face. Somewhere, I could feel my mother cringing and tsking.

"So I hear," said Liz. "How about after breakfast?"

I finished chewing the toast before I answered. "I'm sure I'll need another cup of coffee," I said. "Then I'll have to digest. And get some work clothes on. Then I'll—"

"Just be here in an hour," she said and hung up.

The exchange made me smile. I didn't much care for Ernie Chin, but at least I liked his lawyer.

* * *

No other potential clients queued up outside my door after breakfast. I might as well hear what Liz and Ernie had to say. I got dressed, putting on a pair of gray chinos and a maroon button-down shirt. An hour and eight minutes later, I walked into Baltimore City Office of the Public Defender. Two minutes after, a receptionist talking into a headset mic pointed me to Liz Fleming's door.

"You're late," came the reply when I knocked.

I opened to find a desk chewing up most of the square footage, and the other furnishings made moving and turning around an adventure. Ernie sat in one of two shopworn chairs. I couldn't tell which looked more drab and lifeless. Bags hung under his eyes, his hair begged for a comb, and he didn't even acknowledge me when I walked in. Liz Fleming, on the other hand, sized me up as I entered. She wore a sharp navy suit. Her long brown hair framed a pretty face and got a mild taming from a beret above her left ear. I pegged her around my age and hoped for her sake she hadn't been in this job since college. Liz propped her feet on the desk, forcing her skirt farther up her legs. The legs told me she ran to keep in shape. I liked what I saw.

"Close the door," she said. I did and sat in the other old chair. Liz kept her desk moderately organized. No stacks of papers littered it, but a neat freak would still look upon it and despair. I chalked it up to her caseload, which must border on the Herculean. "You're late," she repeated.

"I'm always late," I said.

"I can't be late," said Liz.

"Did you call me here to compare punctuality?"

"For him." She nodded toward Ernie, who glanced at both of us but said nothing.

"I've already told him no twice."

"Maybe the third time is the charm, then. I'm going to ask again."

"Your office must have investigators," I said.

"We do," Liz said, "and they're stretched even thinner than the lawyers."

"And now you want my help."

"Ernie, can you give us a minute? I'll have the receptionist send you back when we're done."

Roused from his reverie, he grunted, stood, and trudged out of the room.

"Thanks . . . I didn't want to call him an idiot a third time," I said after he left.

"What's your story?" Liz said, narrowing hazel eyes.

"I'm smart, handsome, and good at my job. What else do you want to know?"

"You showed up on the scene a couple months ago. I've read about your cases. You don't charge your clients?" I shook my head. "What's that about?"

"A man needs a little mystery," I said. Bonus: it sounded better than the truth. I worked for my parents' foundation, and they paid me to solve cases for people who lacked any other recourse. Liz might appreciate my forced altruism, but I figured being vague was the better play.

"Humor me," said Liz.

"I humored you when I came down here."

She picked up a coffee mug that had been hiding behind her laptop and took a drink. It made her grimace. "I suppose you did," she said. "Still, I don't know about you. You weren't a cop, you weren't in the military, but now you're a PI."

"I'm sure the articles covered this. I haven't exactly hidden from the press."

"I was just wondering if you had anything to add. You know. . . something that may not have made it into the puff pieces."

"Those puff pieces have allowed me to help several people."

"If you say so."

"If you think I'm some random guy," I said, "why do you want me to help with Ernie's case?"

"I don't have much of a choice," Liz said. "Considering that he confessed, this case isn't getting a lot of resources. My boss didn't give me an investigator, and none of them have the time to pitch in."

"So I'm your last resort."

"Basically."

"Something a guy loves to hear from a girl," I said.

Liz gave a nice smile at my comment. It put dimples in her cheeks and added warmth to her eyes. "Is that a yes?"

I didn't want this case, but I didn't have any other prospects. And Ernie, dumb as he acted, was the kind of person my parents wanted me to help when they wrangled me into this. "Sure."

"Great," Liz said. She smiled again. I couldn't manage a full one in return. Liz would have to settle for the low-wattage version. Unperturbed, she pushed a button on her phone. "Can you send Ernie back in?"

Liz had kept her feet on the desk. I took

another look at her legs, couching it in a scan of the room. They were the kind whoever invented the skirt kept in mind when first putting scissors to fabric. When Ernie walked in, I caught Liz looking at me. She glanced away as her client took his seat.

We went over everything again. Ernie's story didn't change. After he told it again, I posed a question. "I read your blog. Lots of good information in there. Where did you get it?"

"I always try to have stuff the press doesn't," Ernie said.

"Not an answer," I said.

Ernie frowned and thought about it. "I have a source."

I expected more, but he said nothing else. "Who?"

"I can't give up my source."

"Ernie, that's not going to help you," said Liz.

"You're not a goddamn journalist," I said. "You're an idiot with a blog. Congratulations on being a well-informed idiot. Now tell us who gave you the information."

He shook his head. "I can't."

Liz sighed. "This isn't going to be easy."

"I've learned it never is," I said.

CHAPTER 2

I SHARED COFFEE WITH MY COUSIN RICH AT HIS desk in the squad room. He somehow chokes down the swill standing in for coffee in the Baltimore Police Department, but today, I spared him by bringing him something fit for human consumption. Rich spent several years in uniform and got his detective's shield around the time I got my license. The fact he earned two commendations on my cases in the same short time was a coincidence to Rich (and a source of amusement to me).

"You're working for the blogger?" said Rich.

"I think so," I said.

"You haven't decided yet?"

"He has a public defender. I guess I'm technically working for her."

Rich smirked. "Liz Fleming?"

"Yes," I said.

He sipped his coffee. "Good-looking woman."

"I noticed." I remembered Liz's legs stretched out with her feet on her desk. It was a pleasant recollection.

"I'm sure you did," Rich said.

"Are you insinuating I agreed to help because she's pretty?"

"I'm not *insinuating* anything."

I grinned. "Okay, let's just say being a good-looking woman helps."

Rich drank some more of his coffee. So did I. A few cops moved about the room. This was a new squad bay with open-concept seating and glass walls for the few offices. Only the interrogation rooms could not boast of the transparency loved by consultants and funded by taxpayers. I wondered how many of my tax dollars the BPD sacrificed for this extravagance.

"Your guy did it," Rich said after a few minutes.

"What makes you so sure?"

"His statement. He mentioned a few things we didn't release to the papers."

"Maybe he talked to the reporters," I said.

"And maybe he stabbed the vic a dozen times in the chest."

I shook my head. "Ernie's a moron, but he's an honest one. He's not a killer."

"You're so certain."

"I have a pretty good record of being right."

"How many cases have you worked?" Rich said with a chuckle. "Four?"

"Six."

"You took statistics in college, didn't you?"

"I know," I said, "small sample size. What about my twenty-eight years of brilliance?"

"Not convincing enough. Reporters know when we're leaving something out strategically. Even the younger ones get it. They're not going to blab it to some asshole with a blog."

"Ernie's written some good pieces. Someone has to be telling him something."

"Or he's a killer," said Rich.

"He's written about a bunch of murders."

"So?"

"So do you think a tubby college student is a serial killer?" I said.

"Of course not."

I smiled and raised my cup toward Rich. "Not a killer."

Rich rolled his eyes. "Find proof he didn't do it, then."

"You realize the legal system works the other way, right?"

"Don't lecture me on the system," Rich said. "You do as much as you can to not be a part of it."

"And so far," I said, "I've been successful."

We bantered a little more until our cups were empty, and Rich said he had work to get back to. I returned to my car. Ernie wasn't a killer. I knew it but couldn't prove it. Could the state's attorney prove he was? I saw how Ernie knowing intimate details of murders might trouble the police. He claimed a source but wouldn't budge on unmasking said source. I knew he wasn't a killer.

But was I right?

* * *

ERNEST CHIN ENTERED the world twenty years ago in Baltimore, born to a Chinese immigrant father and a Caucasian mother of US nationality. Nothing about his history jumped out as a red flag. Ernie breezed through his first dozen years of school and got a scholarship to Hopkins, where he studied civil engineering. He completed three semesters before steering his life off the rails. Perhaps he could put his municipal work knowledge to use and suggest some design improvements for the roads around Central Booking.

Somewhere along the way, Ernie became fascinated with murder, and there were certainly enough in Baltimore to gain his attention. His popular blog cited the Freddie Gray incident as a "catalyst" for him, and the *Serial* podcast as an "inspiration." I almost flew home from Hong Kong when the aftermath of Freddie Gray's death exploded onto the national consciousness, as well as onto Chinese news broadcasts. I felt sympathetic toward the protesters, but my sympathy diminished as buildings burned. Seeing my city in flames was difficult. I was angry and sullen for a few days, and only a new spate of work with my hacker friends pulled me out of it. So if Ernie cited Freddie Gray as a catalyst, I could understand.

What I couldn't understand was Ernie's moronic confession. His interest in murder and his blog were mentioned in all the news stories and TV segments. Traffic to his site spiked. Even old posts saw new comments, though many were uncharitable. If Ernie monetized his traffic—and he seemed savvy enough to do so—then he collected even more money in the last few days.

A lot of good it would do him in prison.

Ernie seemed to think the police would not take his confession seriously. The opposite happened. Because Ernie knew a lot about the murder, the BPD detained him after he confessed. I didn't think he was a killer, but how would I prove his innocence? The state's attorney may come to realize the circumstantial nature of the case. Or he may not, and Ernie might get indicted and face a trial. I once heard someone say you could get a ham sandwich indicted for being eaten. I hoped Ernie's odds were better.

All this for publicity and blog traffic.

A large part of me still thought Ernie was an

idiot and deserved an idiot's fate. However, I threw my lot in with him and Liz Fleming. I needed to prove Ernie was just a cretin and not a killer. To do it, I would need to look into the murder victim and figure out who gave Ernie all the insider information responsible for his current accommodations.

As I prepared to unearth his source, I was struck by the similarity to Alice's mad tumble into a deep and labyrinthine rabbit hole. As if the murder victim checked a watch from the pocket of a waistcoat, I followed his white ghost.

* * *

THE BPD HAD a nice case file going. I know because I could sit in my office and read it. During my first case two months ago, Rich had left me unsupervised at his PC. People like me don't need much time to profit from such a mistake. Armed with his IP and hardware addresses, I fingerprinted the BPD's network, found the important resources, and mimicked their IP and hardware addressing on one of my virtual machines. The BPD's network accepted the machine as one of its own. I had never seen a sign they noticed the intrusion.

Dave Waugh's violent end involved more than a dozen stab wounds to his upper body. The crime scene photos showed him in a red shirt beginning its sartorial life as a much lighter color. He was found a block from St. Mark's Catholic Church, a venerable building I recalled looking dated in my youth. The church had a website of equally ancient design, and I snagged their member list in under a minute. Dave or David Waugh did not appear on it. Nothing on his social media pages showed any affiliation with a religion.

I probed Waugh's life. He hailed from Phoenix, born there twenty-nine years ago, a year older than I am. I stared at my screen as I pondered mortality at such a young age. Dave had been stabbed over twelve times. His was a normal job, working as an assistant manager at Staples. Mine was far more dangerous. My parents enrolled me in martial arts classes at eleven, after I got my ass handed to me by a bully. I kept up my studies and could take care of myself in a fight. Knives, however, were an equalizer. Maybe Dave possessed similar training. One lucky swing or stab and none of it mattered.

I shook myself out of these morose thoughts. Waugh lived an unremarkable life. I couldn't find much on his youth in Phoenix. He left after his junior year of college and finished his degree at Towson. Since then, he held a handful of jobs with the current one marking the longest time he spent in any of them. Nothing about him stood out as remarkable, and the only thing I found interesting was the spotty history of his youth.

Waugh sustained a large social media presence,

and I dove into it. He had been especially active on Twitter, retweeting a lot of articles and linking to some of his own blog posts. Great—another blogger. This guy should serve as a lesson for Ernie. I followed a bunch of Dave's retweets. They referenced the Catholic church in various uncharitable ways. A common theme emerged after a few: sexual abuse by priests. Waugh's blog posts covered the same subject matter, though with less detachment and more invective.

And he had been found murdered a stone's throw from a Catholic church.

I couldn't consider it a coincidence.

* * *

THE NEXT MORNING, I drove to St. Mark's. I timed my arrival when morning service let out. A few people filed out as I walked up the steps. The building's cornerstone proclaimed 1921. I believed it. The church needed an extended collection drive to power wash and spruce up the exterior. I held the door for a woman who looked to be in her eighties. She smiled and said, "God bless you" as she left. I just smiled and refrained from telling her I hadn't sneezed.

The small vestibule led to heavy double doors, which opened into the church proper. The height of church interiors always impressed me. Even if this wasn't the painted heights of the Sistine Chapel, someone had to get up there and hang the lights. Even smaller churches like St. Mark's boasted very high ceilings. Soft organ music played as I walked down the center aisle. Several of the dark brown pews needed refurbishing, too. I guessed the church would seat about two hundred fifty worshipers. Votive candles burned in alcoves, and the small flames danced in nearby stained glass windows. Even with the shopworn exterior, St. Mark's still had a nice interior identifying it as a Catholic church. I saw the priest talking to an elderly man. I waited near the first pew.

After a minute, the old man bid the priest farewell. I recognized Father Lawrence Toohey from the church's website; he turned to me and offered a tentative smile. I placed him at about fifty, with black hair turning to a dignified gray. He was balding on top, stood about five-ten, and stayed slender into his middle years. "Interested in joining the parish?" he said.

"Not right now," I said. "Is there someplace we might talk?"

The priest held his arms wide. "Only God will overhear us in here." He gestured toward the first pew. I moved down a few feet and sat, leaving Father Lawrence room. He seated himself about a foot away. "Is something troubling you?"

I showed him my ID. "You can probably figure out why I'm here."

He nodded. "That poor man."

"What can you tell me about him?"

The priest sighed. "I barely knew him. He'd come around a few times in the last month or so."

"Was he a parishioner?" I said.

"No, but we don't discriminate. This is a house of God, not a club."

"Father Lawrence, it's—"

"Please," he said, "call me Father Larry. Everyone does."

"All right. You said Dave Waugh came around a few times. Did he attend mass?"

"At least once, yes."

"What was he doing the other times?"

"I don't know. Sitting in the pews, mostly. At first, I thought he was homeless."

"He didn't come for confession?" I said.

"I offered to hear it," said Father Larry. "He . . . wouldn't take me up on it."

"Did he say why?"

"He said he didn't have much to confess."

I would have probably said the same. Of course, my litany of sins to confess would monopolize a priest's time. "You didn't find that odd?" I said.

Father Larry shrugged. "Not everyone wants to confess."

"Some have more need of it than others."

"True," Father Larry said with small smile. "All I can do is ask. People need to be willing to receive a sacrament."

"Did you know Dave Waugh was an active blogger?"

"We barely talked. I never asked him what he did."

"He talked a lot about sexual abuse by priests."

"A sad part of our history," Father Larry said, shaking his head. "I'd like to think the Catholic Church has gotten rid of the bad seeds, if you will."

I looked around for a moment. No one else was in the church. The organist had left. No one came out from the sacristy. "Are you the only priest here?" I said.

"For now."

"For now?"

"We're working on some fundraising," Father Larry said. "It will take a while, but we'd like to build a bigger church—the structure and the congregation to fill it. If we can, I'm sure we'd get at least one more priest."

"How would someone writing about priests abusing boys affect your fundraising?"

"I can't imagine it would help," he said, frowning. "But if you're implying—"

"I'm not implying anything, Father. Just asking questions."

"Yes. Well, since I am the only priest here, I have some duties to attend to."

"Of course."

Father Larry stood and walked out of the pew. "Let me know if you need anything else," he said. "Dave seemed . . . troubled, but I think he was a good man."

"I'm sure I'll be in touch," I said.

CHAPTER 3

Something didn't sit right with me after my chat with Father Larry. He said he knew Dave Waugh but not too well, and still felt bad he died. I didn't have a problem with the last part; in fact, it seemed like a priestly thing to say. The other part bothered me. I looked at Dave Waugh's address. He lived four miles from St. Mark's church. Presuming he was Catholic, plenty of churches stood closer to his apartment than St. Mark's.

Nothing in his history suggested an affiliation with any specific church, but before, I'd only skimmed his blog. Now I scrutinized it. Its title, *We are the Violets*, sort of made sense, trying to answer the question posed in the title of the Auberon Waugh book. It made me wonder if the surname came with his birth certificate or got chiseled onto something later. Unlike Ernie's made-up *murderphiles* word, Dave's title choice didn't shake my faith in the English language. Waugh updated his blog a couple times a week, often with stories of priests abusing someone. After a period of decline, reports of abuse trended upward recently in nearby dioceses. Dave's entries contained a little investigating, and some of his posts featured interviews with victims or their families.

I wondered—and suspected—why Dave was such a crusader in this area, but his blog never delved into his own details. He reported on other people's stories, with one curious omission from the most current updates: names. In older cases, where the events and parties were known, the blogs called out the priests. Newer posts didn't name names, however. Maybe a lawyer told him not to identify someone who hadn't been charged or convicted of a crime. Dave's site looked like he'd put some effort into assembling it. Posts were indexed by subject, the layout and theme made sense for the grim subject matter, and comments were lively.

With nothing else on the blog, I dug deeper. Again, I ran into the issue that Dave Waugh didn't have much of a life history before he turned eighteen. Several things could cause this. He could have been home-schooled, thus avoiding traditional school records. He could have lived a boring life. He could have grown up overseas. Or he could have changed his name or identity. Spurred by the literary last name, I latched onto the last one and ran with it.

Public records searches yield only so much information. The good stuff isn't available from a common web search, at least not for free. I never let such concerns deter me, however. Computers are simple machines, and the things protecting them are often equally simple. I learned the science of computers in college. I developed the art of compromising them on my own, refined by my time in Hong Kong.

Dave Waugh's social security number got issued when he was eighteen. He was not an immigrant receiving a number upon completing the citizenship class. It took some more digging to find out the SSN replaced an older one, issued at birth to Donald Watson. Now I had a better starting point. Dave Waugh's past started where Donald Watson's ended.

Donald was a good student and grew up in a Catholic family in Phoenix. They belonged to St. Isaac's. Young Donald served as an altar boy for about six years. He stopped his service, and his family stopped going to St. Isaac's when a priest there was accused of molesting the altar boys. It only took me a minute to find the priest's name.

Lawrence Toohey.

* * *

I WENT BACK TO ST. Mark's. The church itself was empty, so I wandered into the attached rectory. The attendant there, a high school boy, directed me to Father Larry's office. The door was open a crack. I knocked and entered when directed.

"Mr. Ferguson," Father Larry said, a small frown pulling his eyebrows down. "What brings you back so soon?"

"May I sit?" I pointed to one of the two wooden chairs in front of his desk.

"Please."

I took the left chair. Father Larry's office was about the size of mine, which was really my second bedroom. For a rectory, I expected larger. The bookshelf behind him showed many books on religion and theology and an almost equal number about sports. Father Larry's degrees, including a master's in theology, hung on the wall to his right.

"Did something urgent come up?" the priest said.

"I don't know if I'd call it urgent," I said, "but it's interesting and troubling."

"What do you mean?"

"What did you call it, Father Larry? 'A sad part of our history,' I think it was."

"You mean the priests who . . . harmed those boys."

"I mean you," I said.

"Me?" Father Larry must have practiced the taken aback look. He delivered a decent one.

"You said Dave Waugh came around a few times."

"Yes," said Father Larry.

"Did he look familiar to you at all?"

"I don't know." The priest shrugged. Furrows affixed themselves to his brow and threatened never to leave. "I guess. Maybe he just had one of those faces."

"Maybe. Or maybe Dave Waugh was really Donald Watson." I watched Father Larry for a reaction. None came.

"I don't know the name."

"Sure you do. You knew him back in Phoenix. From what I've read, you knew him biblically."

Father Larry's frown deepened, but he didn't give any other reaction. If I didn't find him so slimy, I might have been impressed. "I still don't know what you're talking about," he said.

"Let me guess," I said, "records were sealed?" Father Larry didn't say anything, so I continued. "And you were never charged with a crime while church officials moved you into a teaching role for ten years. Maybe they figured seminary students were too old for you."

"Now you're simply being crass."

"True. However, after a decade of teaching,

your record got scrubbed clean, and you were back in front of congregations."

"I don't know what you're after here," said Father Larry. "Maybe you have something against priests. Whatever you think of me, though, I'm not a murderer." He stared at me the entire time he said it. While he looked annoyed, he sat still and didn't yell.

"I think you might be telling the truth," I said.

"I am."

"But what if your parishioners found out about the past?"

"You do know priests aren't wealthy, Mr. Ferguson? I don't think your extortion will get you very far."

"Extortion implies I want something from you, Father."

"Why ask the question, then?" he said.

"Did it make you angry?"

"I am a fallible man."

"Angry enough to want to, say, stab me twelve times in the chest?"

Father Larry did a double-take and sat back in his chair. "You think I killed Dave?"

"He blogged about what happened," I said. "There are two good things in this for you and your parish: he hadn't named any names yet, and no one picked up the story. I don't know how long the second one will last, especially with this whole mess back in the news."

I waited while Father Larry took a couple of deep breaths. "I told you, Mr. Ferguson. I am a fallible man. I'm sure I have let God down in the past, but I meant it when I said I'm not a killer."

"You didn't recognize Dave Waugh as Donald Watson?"

"Not at all . . . and he never said anything about it."

I believed him. Father Larry made an excellent suspect. He had motive; just because no one picked up Dave Waugh's story now didn't mean someone couldn't carry it forward later. Maybe Dave kept notes and retained a list of names to reveal in future blogs. While the abuse he chronicled was in the past, I didn't think St. Mark's parishioners--or any, for that matter--would be forgiving once the truth got thrust into the spotlight. Motive alone was never enough. If I wanted to prove Ernie Chin's innocence, I would need a better suspect.

"I think you're being honest, Father," I said. "But the police would tell you you're a person of interest here. I may need to talk to you again."

"I'll tell you the truth," said Father Larry, "I hope you don't. But I want to see the killer found. It sounds like Dave has been through enough in this life. I hope he has found peace in the next one."

I didn't have much to say in reply, so I left.

* * *

I DROVE BACK to my apartment in Fells Point. It was enough in the old part so getting there required a brief drive on cobblestone streets. However, like most places in Fells Point, a trip down the block revealed a pleasant mix of retro and modern. My building looked newer than it was thanks to careful renovations inside and out. As I approached the front, I saw two large men who were not part of the renovation committee. They stood near the front door with their arms crossed. Both were taller and wider than me. One's blond spiky hair made him look ridiculous; the other sported a shaved head. I felt my pulse jump a bit at the impending fight. Even though I had years of training, a situation like this always drove the beats per minute a little higher. When the reaction stopped, I would be worried.

"Guys, I gave at the office," I said.

"Maybe we're here to ask you to give blood," the blond said.

"Pretty clever," I said, and it was. I didn't think either of them had a good quip in them.

"Enough chit-chat," the other one said. "You know why we're here?"

"You're collecting for TDA."

"The fuck is TDA?"

"Two Dumb Assholes," I said.

Blondie snickered, which earned him a scowl from his clean-pated compatriot. "Listen up, prick," Shaved Head said, "you been asking a lot of questions."

Of a priest, I thought. Would Father Larry call a couple of goons on me? How many priests kept assholes like these two in their contacts lists? "Nature of my job," I said.

"Maybe you should consider a career change."

"You first."

"I don't think he's gonna play ball," the blond one said.

"Let's find out. You gonna keep asking questions?"

"Who wants to know?" I said.

"You ain't playing ball," Baldy said, and he threw a right hook. It came in faster than I would have given him credit for, but I still had plenty of time to block it. While he wound up his left hand, Blondie strode closer. I didn't want to tangle with both of them at once. Their combined size and muscle could give them the edge. I blocked Baldy's left, took a step forward, and kicked his partner square in the balls. His eyes threatened to bulge out of his head as he folded in half and pitched forward.

The other tried to grab me in a headlock, but I slid away. He hit me with a jab in the side as I did. Even though he couldn't get a lot of power behind the punch, it still hurt. He gave me a wolfish grin.

I needed to end this before the goon on the sidewalk recovered. He coughed and raised himself to all fours. When the clean-shaven goon tried another right hook, I hit him with a quick right jab, then a series of rapid body blows. It staggered him enough to give me the chance to punt the spiky blond head and put it on the concrete again. Baldy recovered, and I launched a right kick at his midsection, but he blocked it and grabbed my ankle. There were a lot of ways this could end poorly. I pushed off with my left foot, leaned back, and put what I could into another kick. It took him in the thigh. The impact got him to let go, and I fell to the pavement.

As my bald adversary came forward again, I rose to a crouch. He launched a few punches, trying to end the fight in one swing. I turned them all aside. He kept the blows coming. Blocking them wasn't a challenge. I held a good base and balance. After a few more, punches slowed, and I heard my foe breathing hard. Turning aside a haymaker, I landed a solid right cross to the goon's midsection. He doubled over as I stood up. I grabbed the collar of his shirt, elbowed him twice in the head, then drove my knee into his face. His bald head snapped back, and he fell not far from his unconscious blond friend.

"You were right," I said. "Tell whoever sent you I'm not playing ball."

The would-be bully tried to say something, but it got lost in a sea of coughs and mumbles.

"I'm calling the cops. They have a precinct not far from here. You've probably got about three minutes to collect your buddy and fuck off."

He muttered something uncharitable, so I kicked him in the face. Then I went inside and called the police.

CHAPTER 4

THE NEXT MORNING, I WALKED INTO RICH's precinct. He sat at his desk, staring at his monitor. "Maybe this will help," I said, setting a fresh coffee on the desk before him.

Rich sniffed and smiled. "Smells good."

"And it saves you from drinking the sewage they call coffee here."

"Tastes good, too," he said after taking a drink.

"Light roast," I said. "The way you were mesmerized by your screen, it looks like you could use the boost."

Rich took a big swig. He wore a gray suit with a white shirt and a red tie. Knowing Rich, he probably owned ten sets of coats with pants in five pairs —one to wear while its twin spent quality time with the dry cleaner. Wearing the Friday outfit on a Thursday was not calculus Rich could do. His suit looked off the rack, but it was one I would have owned. Rich didn't spend as much time or money on clothes as I did, but he dressed well. Like any consumer with a whit of fashion sense, he never shopped those horrific buy-three-for-$200 sales.

"What brings you by?" Rich said. "I presume you didn't come in merely to give me coffee."

"The Dave Waugh case," I said.

"Still trying to get your boy off the hook?"

"Did you talk to the priest?"

"You think a priest killed him?"

I sipped my vanilla latte. "Did you know the priest was accused of abusing Dave years ago?"

Rich frowned. "No, I didn't."

"Did you talk to him?"

"A couple of uniforms did," Rich said. "He didn't say anything we felt needed following up."

"Good thing you have me here to lead you down the right path," I said.

"Even if the priest did abuse this guy years ago, it doesn't mean he killed him now." Rich went back to his screen. The BPD had Ernie in custody after his stupid phony confession. Rich needed more convincing.

"I talked to the priest twice," I said. "After the second time, a couple goons ambushed me outside my building."

Rich looked at his screen another few seconds, then shifted back to me. "So not only did the priest kill the vic, he also keeps goons in his Rolodex?"

"You *would* call it a Rolodex."

"Do you know what a Rolodex is?" Rich said with an amused smile.

"Sure," I said. "I've watched *Antiques Roadshow*."

"Touché." Rich gave a chuckle.

"You don't find it odd? I talk to the priest a second time, and then a couple of assholes are trying to get me to back off?"

Rich consulted his screen again. "I thought I saw something about two guys getting picked up near your building."

"If you mean on the front steps, yes."

"You went to church when you were a kid," Rich said. I nodded. "So did I. I still go for Christmas and Easter. It's just . . ."

". . . hard for you to think a priest is a killer?" I said.

"Yeah."

"Maybe he's not. Maybe the strong-arm types he called on me are the ones who killed Dave Waugh."

"Not much difference legally," Rich said.

"I don't know a ton about the priest yet," I said, "but I know this much . . . he was in Phoenix years ago. If you looked into Dave Waugh, you noticed he doesn't have much of a history. It's because he was born Donald Watson, who was 'allegedly' the victim of sexual abuse at the hands of Father

Lawrence Toohey. I'm sure you recall the Catholic Church had some problems in this area, and now they do again. Father Larry was one of them. He was never charged with a crime, but he got moved from a parish to teaching at the seminary for ten years. Then he gets the tabula rasa treatment and ends up here in Baltimore."

Rich said, "Where Dave Waugh moved years ago."

"Yes."

"I don't know." Rich frowned. "There's a lot of circumstantial and coincidental in there."

"Seems like enough to cast reasonable doubt on Ernie Chin stabbing Waugh."

"Have you been to the public defender yet?"

"She's my next stop," I said.

"All right," Rich said with a nod. "I'll look into it."

"You shouldn't have to look too hard to see Ernie is no killer."

Rich sipped his coffee. "Be careful how hard you look. If you piss someone off again, they might send more than two goons."

"I'll be ready," I said.

* * *

LIKE I SAID I WOULD, I went to see Liz Fleming after I talked to Rich. I didn't have a coffee for her, so I finished my latte before I walked into her office. She sat behind her desk, wearing an unfortunately conservative white shirt and blue blazer. "Got something for me?" she said.

"Good morning to you, too," I eased into one of her lousy guest chairs.

Liz flashed the kind of patient smile I became used to seeing in school. "Good morning. Got something for me?"

"I do." I told her about my visits to Father Larry, the history between him and Dave Waugh, and the welcoming committee outside my building.

"Are you all right?" Liz said. She kicked her feet up onto the desk. Her blazer was part of a pantsuit. I tried to hide my disappointment, but her smirk told me I hadn't.

"Neither rain, nor sleet, nor amateur legbreakers will keep me from my appointed rounds," I said.

Liz smiled. Her eyes brightened and dimples appeared in her cheeks. It was the kind of face a man could get used to seeing. "That's good to know."

"So what does this mean for Ernie?"

"It helps," Liz said. "I just don't think it helps immediately. He confessed. That means something. You've given me good information to work with, but there's a process. We need to investigate it."

"It's not reasonable doubt?" I said.

"It helps toward that, but it's an issue for a trial. I'd like to prevent this case from getting to that point."

"You're saying I need to pin something on the priest."

"Or whoever sent those guys after you," said Liz.

"Why does no one think a priest could have done it?" I said.

Liz shrugged. "Why do you seem convinced that he did?"

"The history between him and Dave."

"OK, so he had a motive."

"And means. Everyone has a knife. And opportunity . . . Waugh came by the church a couple of times."

"Then you need to make it stick," Liz said.

"No, making it stick is your job," I said. "I only need to bring you enough to make it happen."

She nodded. "You really think the priest did it?"

"I think it's not a big leap from sexually abusing altar boys to stabbing people," I said.

"The defense would say most sex abusers aren't violent like that," Liz pointed out.

"Then let them say it at his trial."

"Get me to that point."

"I will," I said.

CHAPTER 5

I GOT HOME AND FOUND NO MORE ENFORCERS waiting for me. The elevator and my floor were similarly clear. Once back in my office, I resumed work. I'd gathered the big-picture details about Father Larry. More had to be there. Between church records and whatever the Phoenix police may have discovered, I wanted to unearth enough to spring Ernie. I made a mental note not to take cases from any more idiots. Possible cheating spouses already topped the blacklist. Stupid people creating their own problems now made the second entry.

The Catholic Church's private records were easy to access. They must not have thought themselves big targets for hackers—perhaps damnation proved a powerful deterrent. I gained access to the full personnel records in a matter of minutes. Father Larry's file said he was fifty-two. He got his bachelor's in theology and then entered the seminary. From there, he spent two years as a deacon before becoming ordained twenty-eight years ago. The first decade of his career in the cloth saw him serve at two parishes. No scandals or issues followed him. The ecclesiastical equivalent of performance reviews said he was a good and popular priest, well-liked by young and old.

Fifteen years ago, the first irregularity appeared. Eight months after arriving at Holy Redeemer in Phoenix, Father Larry got sent to St. Joseph's. His file mentioned "irregular behavior" with the youth of the parish, citing two parent complaints. Neither accused him of sexual abuse, however. The move must have been precautionary, an attempt to head off any more bad publicity on the priests-and-young-boys front.

A year later, it happened again.

This time, Father Larry got shipped from St. Joseph's in Phoenix to St. Matthew's in Casa Grande. I never heard of Casa Grande, so I consulted the Oracle of Google Maps. It sat about an hour outside of Phoenix, breaking up a large swath of desert, and would be considered a much less prestigious assignment, if priests cared about such a thing. The Phoenix PD didn't have much better security than the Catholic Church. Maybe they could confess to using shoddy IT contractors. I checked around the date Father Larry got sent to

Casa Grande. The PPD investigated an incident at St. Joseph's, involving an unnamed minor and one Father Lawrence Toohey. I read the detective's notes. He thought Father Larry was guilty but couldn't make the case against him. No charges got filed.

After two uneventful years in Casa Grande, Father Larry got called back up to the big leagues in Phoenix, this time back at Holy Redeemer. There, he met Donald Watson and another altar boy. The PPD opened another investigation. This time, a different detective felt the same way about Father Larry's guilt and experienced the same luck building the case. Again, no charges filed. Father Larry got exiled to the seminary, where he spent the next ten years teaching and getting his master's. Diocese records contained a few notes about "inappropriate relationships with altar boys" but never mentioned abuse. Even if someone lawfully accessed the files, nothing stated Father Larry was an abuser in clear, explicit terms. Reaching such a conclusion required simple inferences, but my feeling was defense lawyers could argue against those simple inferences if something ever made it to court.

During Father Larry's ten years at the seminary, no one reported any incidents. His master record still contained all the issues from the past, but the more compact HR record individual churches saw—and which I saw at first—didn't mention anything. *Tabula rasa,* a clean slate. Pastors and monsignors were unlikely to ask about things like sexual abuse, and I didn't know if they could even see the master files. The church maintained a system to protect their own, regardless if those men deserved protection. I wondered if they would ever learn.

Now I knew more about Father Larry. He was definitely a sex offender, even if the Phoenix police couldn't even charge him with it. Like many guilty men, he could point to the lack of charges against him and exclaim his innocence. Rich's comment stuck with me, however: none of this meant Father Larry killed Dave Waugh. And none of it meant he sicced goons on me. I still needed to make those accusations stand up.

* * *

I STILL LIKED Father Larry for the stabbing. Part of my suspicions was the absence of any other credible suspect. Another part was how well he fit into the role of killer. None of the circumstantial evidence meant he did it, of course, but I didn't have anyone else to investigate. So I drove back to St. Mark's.

The church was open. I walked in and sat in the back pew. Father Larry stood about halfway down the aisle, his back to me, talking to a man who wore a suit I would have been proud to own. Most of the lights were off, so I couldn't discern much more, but great suits are easy to spot in any light. To my right, at the other end of the pew, another man sat. He also watched Father Larry and the mystery man talk. A couple minutes later, the two shook hands. The well-dressed man walked toward the back of the church. The fellow at the end of the pew stood and joined him on the way out.

Father Larry hadn't noticed me. He took a wooden wick in his left hand, held it to the flame of a votive candle, and lit another. I glanced around. A handful of other people sat in pews, not paying attention to Father Larry or me. I took out my phone and used a secure remote protocol called SSH to connect to my server at home. I opened the crime scene photos and zoomed in on them. I'm neither a cop nor a medical examiner—and I considered saying a quick prayer of thanks for both —but the angle of the stab wounds suggested a left-handed attacker.

Another mark against Father Larry.

I remained in the pew. After a minute, Father Larry turned. His grimace told me he noticed me even in the dim lighting. He walked toward me, pausing for a moment to exchange pleasantries with an older lady a few rows ahead of me.

"Mister Ferguson, this is getting ridiculous."

"I know," I said. "I haven't spent this much time in church in years."

"You know what I mean."

"Can't a man sit here and be spiritual?"

"Are you a spiritual man, Mister Ferguson?" said Father Larry.

I shrugged. " It doesn't really matter." I looked around again. Even though the exterior needed work, the interior of St. Mark's remained beautiful. I'd always liked stained glass. "There's something relaxing about sitting in a church."

"Perhaps it's the presence of God."

"Perhaps."

Father Larry followed the sweep of my eyes for a moment. "Was there a reason you came?" he said in a lowered tone. "Other than to toss around accusations, maybe?"

"Who was the man you were talking to a few minutes ago?"

"A parishioner."

"You have many parishioners with bodyguards?" I said. Father Larry didn't say anything. "This isn't a bad neighborhood. Even if it were, the church is mostly empty, so he wouldn't have to walk far to his car."

"We're lucky enough to have a few wealthy parishioners," Father Larry said.

"Wealthy enough to send goons after me?"

My thinly-veiled accusation made Father Larry frown. "I'm not sure what you mean."

"It's pretty simple, Father. Either hiring legbreakers is fine with the current pope, or someone else hired them to take a run at me. I know this pope is seen as pretty progressive, but I doubt it extends quite so far."

"Thank God you weren't hurt."

"Yes," I said with a smirk. "Thank God . . . and years of martial arts."

"Well, I don't think you need to keep coming by. I've told you what I know. This is bordering on harassment."

"Said no innocent person ever."

Father Larry took a deep breath. If we were alone in the church, he might have yelled at me. "I don't know what you're doing here, Mister Ferguson."

"Then you might want to pray for wisdom, Father," I said. "Maybe take a turn in confession."

"Good afternoon." Father Larry walked away.

The man in the suit employed a bodyguard. I wondered who he was and if he sent the legbreakers after me. But why? I didn't see him well in the church lighting, but he didn't look familiar. Did Father Larry ask him to take care of me?

"Maybe I ought to pray for wisdom, too," I said to the mostly-empty church.

* * *

LATER IN THE DAY, Gloria Reading called and inquired as to my plans for the evening. None for me and neither for her. She suggested she come to my place around seven and get dinner; I concurred. Gloria and I enjoyed a relationship of fun and convenience. She came from a similar background but was lucky enough not to work for a living. Gloria played tennis and went to interesting events. If Baltimore had a large enough profile to boast of socialites, she could count herself among them.

With nothing to do for a few hours, I went to the gym. I abused the heavy bag for about a half-hour, lifted some weights, and cycled like I trained for an upcoming race. At home, I showered and ate a small meal to tide me over until dinner. Gloria showed up promptly at seven. I heard her Mercedes rocket-like coupe when it was about a block away. For anyone whose ears didn't split from the sound, the car was helpfully painted bright red to accentuate its rocket-ness.

A few minutes later, Gloria knocked on my apartment door. I opened it and took in the scene. Gloria always looked great, even when she wasn't dressed to the nines. Even her fours and fives were worth an extra glance. She wore light blue jeans appearing painted on and a sweater managing to be loose but still cling to her in all the right places. Her chestnut hair spilled over her shoulders. She smiled as she came in and planted a kiss on me.

We sat on the loveseat and chatted for a few minutes. The conversation inevitably turned to my case. Gloria didn't work, and I thought she found it quaint how I did, but she also listened when I talked about my cases and asked good questions. She never rolled her eyes or blew off my stories. Maybe there was hope for her yet.

"You think the priest did it?" Gloria said after I laid out the details.

"I'm not sure," I said. "At first, I did. He had a good motive."

"But now you don't?"

"He has to be involved somehow."

"It must be weird to go after a priest," said Gloria.

"A little." I gave a slight nod. "No one else thinks he could have anything to do with it. They're all wrapped up in the man-of-the-cloth stuff."

"And you're not."

"There are bad people in every profession. Even if the percentage is lower in the priesthood, they can't all be saints."

Gloria grinned. "Saints?"

"No pun intended," I said.

"It sounds like you've been spending a lot of time in church."

"I have." I looked at Gloria and how her sweater managed to be tight around her breasts and nowhere else. "More than I have in years. I think I need to make up for it."

"Is that so?" Gloria's brown eyes sparkled as she leaned in to kiss me.

"Definitely." I kissed Gloria's neck, and she grabbed my head and wrapped her fingers in my hair.

"What did you have in mind?" Gloria wriggled onto my lap.

"Lots of fornication," I said, recalling the Biblical term.

"I like the way you think," Gloria said as she took her sweater off.

CHAPTER 6

AFTER A NIGHT FILLED WITH THE PROMISED amounts of fornication, I left a sleeping Gloria and hit the streets of Fells Point for a morning run. I made a left on Thames and ran past a lot of shops and eateries, some of which had yet to open. Passing Broadway and the Admiral Fell Inn, I took in the smells of the restaurants open for breakfast and doing their mise en place for lunch. A few cars drove past me. Downtown Baltimore would be playing its soundtrack of car horns and curse words by now, but Fells Point remained quieter. I got near the end of Thames, sprinted up Caroline, and then went to the right on Aliceanna. The aromas from the Blue Moon Cafe almost pulled me in for coffee and a pastry, but I kept going.

When I approached the intersection of Aliceanna and Ann Streets, I noticed two musclemen standing with their arms crossed and blocking the sidewalk. Anyone nearby gave them a wide berth.

Neither looked familiar. How many of these assholes did Father Larry know? I wondered about the man in the nice suit who left with his bodyguard. These two were burlier, but they could all work for the same man. It would make more sense than a priest having a bunch of legbreakers on speed dial. Both men glared at me as I approached since I hadn't slowed.

As I got near them, I feinted toward the one on the right. Then I sprang off my left foot, leaped between them, and drove my left elbow down into the face of the no-neck on the left. He grunted, staggered, and fell. The other threw a punch as I came down. I ducked under it and hit him in the stomach. It only made made him glower more.

He swung again, quicker than I expected. I was unbalanced and while I blocked it, it knocked me on my butt. The first one I put on the sidewalk still covered his face and moaned. I avoided tripping over him as I scooted back to the curb and regained my feet. The second man drifted to my left. Behind me, the prone goon stirred. If he recovered, I would lose whatever advantage I gained by knocking him down.

I ducked under a left from the one on his feet, blocked a right, and gave him a solid jab to the nose. It didn't break the bone, but it did send him stumbling back a couple steps. The guy behind me must have recovered while I did that; the next thing I knew, he wrapped his arms around me from behind. His pal shook off the blow to the face, saw me in the grip of his friend, and smiled.

This could end poorly. I lifted my leg and drove my heel down onto the toes of the man holding me. He yelled in pain and his grip loosened. I slipped out just in time and wormed away from a hard right taking my sore-footed captor flush in the face. Both men cursed as I started away. We already drew a few onlookers, and of course one of them held his phone out, no doubt recording everything while wondering why no one called the authorities. I didn't want any bystander hurt, even the moron who fancied himself a cameraman.

I ran down Ann and checked behind me. Both goons gave chase, but they weren't running full out. I slowed my pace, looked back again, and saw they did the same. They weren't trying to catch me; they were trying to drive me. Probably back to the one place they knew I would go: my apartment building. Where Gloria lay sleeping in my bed.

Using voice commands, I called Gloria's cell. She answered in a sleepy voice. "This is important," I said. "I need you to go downstairs."

"What?" She sounded more alert. "Why, what's wrong?"

"A couple of assholes just tried to assault me."

"Oh, my goodness! Are you all right?"

"I'm fine. Listen. Go downstairs. Act like you're getting the mail or something. Tell me if there are any guys lingering outside."

"OK," Gloria said. "I'm going to throw one of your hoodies on." She paused. I heard clothes rustle. I turned left from Ann onto Lancaster. My building wasn't far. "I'm heading downstairs," Gloria said a moment later. Another pause. Then she said, "Yes, I see two guys. They're really big."

I said, "Did they see you?"

"No, they're looking out at the street."

"Good." I slowed my pace a little more. My pursuers just turned onto Lancaster. They jogged toward me. "Here's what I need you to do: Go back to my apartment. Go into my office, open the desk drawer, and grab a gun."

"A gun?"

"Yes."

"Are they loaded?" said Gloria.

"Of course. Keep your fingers out of the trigger guards, and they can't go off. I don't care which one you get. Just grab one and bring it downstairs."

"C.T., I'm worried about you."

"You won't need to worry so much if you get me a gun," I said.

"I'm working on it." I heard Gloria open a drawer. She was concerned about me. On the one hand, I liked it. On the other, I wondered how it jibed with our relationship of convenience. Right now, I had more pressing concerns. I turned down Wolfe Street. There was one block to Thames, and just beyond that, my building loomed. I could see two figures standing in front of it. By now, they surely saw me.

"I have a gun," Gloria said. "I'm headed back downstairs."

"Good," I said. "Hide it under the hoodie and wait in the lobby. If I need it, I'll let you know."

In my ear, I heard Gloria run down the stairs. A minute later, she said, "I'm in the lobby."

I picked up my pace again as I crossed Thames. Now I could see the two waiting for me were the same pair I dealt with yesterday. If they pulled guns, I would have to keep running and take my chances. I wouldn't involve Gloria in a shootout. As I ran closer, they both took knives out of their coats. While I've always hated fighting people with knives, I preferred them to guns.

"I'm getting close to the building," I said.

"I see you."

"Good. When I approach the stairs, I want you to open the door and throw me the gun. Throw it high so these shitheads can't get it."

"C.T., I'm not sure—"

"Gloria, I need you to do this."

"All right," she said. "I can do it." Waves of apprehension dotted her voice.

I slowed as I approached the stairs. The goons with knives flashed me predatory grins. "Wanna try that shit from yesterday?" one of them said.

"Now," I said.

Behind them, the door opened. The hood of my sweatshirt covering most of her face, Gloria took one step out. Both men turned to look at her. She tossed the gun over their heads. They followed it as it arced over them. I caught it and pointed it at them. Gloria grabbed the .38 revolver. Not my first choice, but it beat a pair of knives.

"How's the saying go about knives and gunfights?" I said. Gloria disappeared back into the lobby.

Both of them frowned and looked at their knives. The one on the right glared, brandished his, and edged forward.

"One more step, and I'll shoot you," I said. He was three paces away. I wouldn't miss. I'd never shot anyone before and didn't relish the possibility, but I also wouldn't let this asshole stab me. Or Gloria.

I considered the possibility they would both rush me. At their current distance, I couldn't shoot both of them in time. One would definitely drop. I stared at the pair as the same math ran through their small brains. It came down to a coinflip. Heads, I live; tails, I get shot isn't appealing calculus.

The wiser goon put a hand on his partner's chest and held him back. I took a few steps to the side, keeping these two on my left. The pair once chasing me now walked down Wolfe. They had to see what happened, so they wouldn't be sticking around. I called the police.

* * *

AFTER I GAVE my statement to the police and they led the two goons away—the first two were long gone by then—I walked back upstairs. During my chat with the police, my hands shook as adrenaline still flowed through my system. I paused outside my apartment door. No more shaking, so I walked in. Gloria sat at the kitchen table, nursing a glass of orange juice. "What the hell was that?"

"Some days, my job is more dangerous than others," I said.

"There were two guys out there with knives." Gloria's eyes widened as she talked. I sympathized. A few months ago, I wouldn't have imagined dealing with threats like theirs. I thought this career would be easy and allow me to work from behind my desk. Each case hammered home how wrong I'd been. Even helping people in China had been simpler—until the Chinese police kicked the door in.

"And two more in the streets," I said. "They seem to have gotten away."

Gloria looked up at me. She held the glass of orange juice. I noticed the liquid trembling. "Were you scared?"

I nodded. "Yes. The day a situation like this doesn't spike my adrenaline, I'm done."

"You're going to keep working?" said Gloria.

"Of course. I've obviously pissed off the right person. Now I need to figure out who it is and how he or she is involved."

"You should give this case up. You could get hurt."

"You can get hurt crossing the street," I said.

"Not the same," Gloria said, shaking her head.

"Fine." I searched for an analogy. "If you lost the first set of a tennis tournament and tweaked your knee in the process, would you forfeit?"

"No. I'd keep playing as long as my knee held up."

"There you go."

"But no one stabbed me in the knee," Gloria said.

I needed a better analogy, and one of my earliest sports memories sprang to mind. "You've heard of Monica Seles, right?" I said.

"You're using that because she got stabbed on the court. Clever."

"I was three or four when it happened . . . one of of the first things I remember from any sport."

"I was too young." Gloria grinned. "I've only heard about it and seen the video. You're older than I am."

"My point is she didn't quit," I said. "An asshole with a knife didn't end her career."

It gave Gloria pause, and she nodded after a moment. "I think I understand. I'd probably understand more if you were competing for millions in prize money."

"If I do this long enough and well enough, there should come a point when I can give it all up."

Gloria smiled. The orange juice stilled in her glass. "That would be nice."

"I chose this career because it seemed like the best of a bad lot. I've come to like it more than I thought, yet I'd still like to walk away after I earn a lot of money."

"As long as you can walk away," Gloria said.

"It's my plan."

"I'm not waiting for you while you hobble along," she said with a grin.

Her joke gave me pause. How did Gloria see our relationship, such as it was, in light of her remark? I chose to ignore it. She could have gotten caught up in the moment. I moved behind Gloria and rubbed her shoulders. "How about you and I walk down the hallway?" I said.

Gloria's chin dropped to her chest, and I swore I heard her purr. "I'm not sure we'll make it there."

We did, but it was close.

* * *

THE WEALTHY PARISHIONER BOTHERED ME. Who brings a bodyguard to church? Why was Father Larry so evasive when I asked a simple question about the mystery man?

As I thought more about the case, I found myself losing certainty in Father Larry as the killer. Even if he did the stabbing, I doubted the goons who twice visited me were deacons doing a priest a solid. Someone with money or influence (or both) must have sent them. My parents might have known who the guy in the church was from my limited description. Then I thought of someone else who was more likely to know.

One of the perks of living in Fells Point is the closeness of Little Italy. On a nice day like today, I could walk there easily. Up Fell Street to Ann, left on Eastern Avenue, and then right on High Street. A mile (and sixteen minutes) later, I walked in the front door of *Il Buon Cibo*, one of the better restaurants in Little Italy.

In addition to being a fine place to catch a meal, *Il Buon Cibo* was a great place to talk to the man who ran organized crime in Baltimore. Tony

Rizzo and my parents had been friends for ages, and the fact they were still friendly meant my mother remained ignorant of his occupation. When I walked in, Tony occupied his usual table near the fireplace. The lunch crowd started to file in. The only tables within ten feet were manned by a pair of enforcers who sized me up as I approached.

"It's OK, boys," Tony said with a smile. "You remember C.T."

Their grunts neither confirmed nor denied their memories of me. "How are you, Tony?" I said. During my three-plus years abroad, Tony lost a good eighty pounds. His face looked a little too thin, though his waistline now inhabited the average range. For a man pushing seventy, he looked to be in good shape. As always, Tony wore a suit, and I knew the tie would be Italian. Probably Versace.

"No complaints," he said, gesturing to the seat across from him. I sat. "What brings you by? You need a free meal?"

"I don't know I need one, but it seems silly to refuse."

Tony chuckled. "You always were practical." He snapped his fingers, and a young waitress appeared. "Take my friend's order."

She spoke to me but also cast an occasional glance at Tony. "Sir, do you need a menu?"

"No, thanks. I'll just have the chicken parm with a side Caesar and an unsweetened tea."

She scribbled on her pad and vanished into the kitchen. After a moment, Tony said, "What really brings you by?"

"I need to know about a mover and shaker."

"Someone I like?"

"I don't know yet," I said. "I didn't see this guy in good lighting." I relayed my imperfect description to Tony. "He was at St. Mark's, and the trip required a bodyguard."

Tony frowned when I mentioned the church. "St. Mark's?"

"You know it?"

"Old Catholic building. They got a priest there now . . . something of a maverick."

I didn't know if Tony referred to Father Larry's dodgy history, so I let it pass. "I'm more interested in a guy wearing a three-thousand-dollar suit and bringing a bodyguard to a church."

"Could be a few people," said Tony.

"Anyone you know well?"

Tony shrugged. "A man like me knows everyone a little." The waitress returned and set my salad and tea on the table. The bowl could have held an entree salad, and the small bowl of dressing would fill half a bottle. The perks of sitting at The Man's table. After she walked away again, Tony continued. "I've heard someone wants to build a new church."

"A new St. Mark's?"

"Yeah. It's old. A new one would be bigger and nicer."

I ruminated on the information over a bite of salad. "And require quite a bit of construction. Which you just might have a piece of."

Tony smiled. "I just might."

"Where's this great new church supposed to be?"

"Right near the old one, I think. I know there's a lot of fundraising going on. The priest is into it, too."

Something else I could look into regarding Father Larry. Before I could say anything else, my main course arrived. The large plate could barely contain it. A family of chickens must have given their lives for the meal, and the sauce came from a half-gallon carton. "I hope this isn't the lunch portion," I said.

"Guests at my table are taken care of," Tony said.

"I appreciate it." So as not to be rude, I ate some chicken parm before continuing the conversation. It was quite good--the bird was cooked well, and the breading was both tasty and light. *Il Buon Cibo* had always made a mean sauce. "You said this guy is fundraising?" Tony nodded. "For the church?" He nodded again. "You get invited to these?"

"I get invited to every fundraiser in the city. Almost never go, though."

"You know when the next St. Mark's one is?"

Tony asked the nearest watchdog for the calendar. He produced some small-bindered monstrosity stuffed with papers and note cards. Tony opened the binder and flipped through it while I ate. Despite the setup looking like a mess, he found the answer after a minute of searching. "You're in luck," he said. "It's tonight."

I smiled around a mouthful of chicken parm. "I have a feeling my parents' foundation will be buying two tickets."

"You're gonna help build a church?"

"I'm trying to find whoever stabbed the guy near the old one."

Tony shook his head. "I don't think the guy I was thinking of is your man."

"Could have been one of his goons," I said, which earned me a glower from Tony's two. "A few of them have come after me."

"And you think they work for him."

"So far, it's him or the priest."

"Probably not the priest."

"Why?"

"All the guys I'm thinking of are real assholes."

I nodded. "Always a good reason."

CHAPTER 7

Gloria let me drive her Mercedes coupe to the fundraiser. Other than the automatic transmission—Gloria never learned to drive a stick—I relished my turn behind the wheel. The engine made going fast very easy. Without even trying, I let the car ease over eighty on the highway, and I knew I could double our speed and the coupe would still have more to give. On top of it all, I felt pretty awesome zooming around in a car shaped and colored like a rocket and wondered if having my mere Lexus parked in her driveway would make Gloria the neighborhood pariah.

We valeted the car and went inside. Years passed since I last visited La Fontaine Bleue. In that time, the place had undergone a total renovation in all but its strange spelling. Marble, granite, and dark wood covered every available surface. Gold trim lent the appearance of opulence even when the material didn't need it. A good crowd gathered in the dining hall. I handed someone our tickets, picked up a couple complimentary glasses of wine, and headed inside.

The VIP tables were predictably close to the stage. I didn't want to sit near them. No point in tipping off Father Larry or his mysterious benefactor to my lurking. Most ringside tables were filled with a bunch of people I didn't know, but a couple I recognized from my parents' foundation shindigs, a familiar goon, and Father Larry. The money man hadn't arrived.

Gloria and I found a spot near the back of the room. We could see the stage, and the classical music playing told us the acoustics would let us hear everything. We made small talk with the other folks at the table, all of whom had at least ten years on us. To my surprise, Gloria chatted easily with everyone. She claimed she didn't relate to people well. Maybe I just needed to take her to more swanky fundraisers.

The wait staff, clad in traditional black and white, brought salads to our group and refilled water glasses all around. The starter dishes boasted of vibrant greens, cherry tomatoes, a lone slice of cucumber, and a bit of onion, all topped with some balsamic dressing. It looked better than it tasted.

After the staff took the salads away, someone got up on stage and made a few opening remarks in a monotone ill-suited for public address. He was Steve Lewis of the St. Mark's Rebuilding Committee, who wished us a lovely meal and promised more comments from more important people later. Gloria and I both needed a second glass of wine to deal with such a riveting agenda.

A few minutes later came the main course. Everyone got a petite filet mignon paired with mashed potatoes and green beans. The first thing I did was cut into the meat. A good steak should be cooked medium. Only barbarians eat it less done, and only philistines cook it longer. The inside showed a little pink, darkening a shade near the center, but no red. A nice medium.

Bits of small talk continued over dinner. Gloria and I both dodged the so-what-do-you-do line of questioning, me by saying I worked in finance, she by saying she decided to go back to school. In a crowd like this, I expect both to get believed with no blowback, and I was right. After the staff collected our dinner plates, they poured coffee.

Steve Lewis took the stage again. "You probably don't want to hear a lot more from me," he said, showing he at least possessed self-awareness. "So let me bring up a man who's been instrumental in our fundraising. We all know him as Father Larry. Please welcome Father Lawrence Toohey!"

The St. Mark's pastor took the microphone. He had swapped his usual priestly attire for black pants, a starched white shirt, and a black tie. Over-all, not much of an improvement. He looked more like a mortician than a priest. Father Larry tapped the mike a couple times and cleared his throat.

"I'm not used to talking without a pulpit," he said to moderate laughter. One man at our table found that endlessly funny for reasons puzzling me and everyone else seated near him. "If you were hoping to hear from Mister V, I'm afraid he's not going to be able to make it tonight." Father Larry kept talking while I held my phone under the table and looked up Mister V. It was my first clue to the identity of the benefactor.

A few minutes of clever Googling didn't come up with anything. My mother would have chided me for using my phone at the dinner table during a speech. No one at the table seemed to notice my distraction or care. Father Larry would have Mister V in his phone, but I was too far away to make a Bluetooth attack work.

"St. Mark's has a strong community," Father Larry said. "We need a new church to grow the community." He kept talking, interrupted a few times by applause. The regular practice he got every weekend made Father Larry a decent speaker, if not a compelling one. The odds of me writing a check to St. Mark's began the evening at zero and remained there.

Father Larry wrapped up his speech a few

minutes later. The wait staff brought out dessert in the form of a mediocre-looking chocolate cake. A few people lined up to shake Father Larry's hands, and some also gave him a check. An idea leapt into my head. "Want to say hello to the good father?" I said to Gloria.

She frowned in surprise. "Not really. He gave a nice speech, but I'm not going to donate."

I handed her my phone. "Can you go talk to him for a minute? Say whatever. He'd recognize me and try to run away, so I'd rather not go."

"What does your phone have to do with anything?" Gloria said. I smiled at her. "Oh." She grinned. "I should have known."

"If this works, I'll start calling you my lovely assistant," I said.

"It'll work." Gloria got up and walked toward the head table. I watched her departure with some interest. A few women in the room opted for gowns, but Gloria was the best dressed of the bunch. I still wanted to rip the dress off her later. She could afford a new one. I bantered with a few people seated nearby as I kept an eye on Gloria. She queued up near Father Larry, exchanged pleasantries, and shook his hand before talking to someone else.

I found out who in a minute when Steve Lewis introduced the fundraising coordinator. Cheryl Olson blushed and waved to the crowd as Lewis sang her praises. She and Gloria talked for a few more minutes before I got my phone back.

"Everything good?" Gloria said as I looked through my Bluetooth jacking app. It connected to other phones with the technology enabled, told me the owner's name, and displayed all contacts, calls, and texts. Bluetooth has an effective range of ten meters, so the app snagged a bunch of other phones. Father Larry's was among them. I deleted the rest without looking at them. Never let it be said I am not a principled hacker.

"I have what I need," I said. "Thanks."

"Sure," Gloria said. "I was talking to the fundraiser. I've seen her at a few things like this before. She does good work."

"You thinking of getting into fundraising?"

"I don't know." Gloria cast her eyes down.

"You'd be good at it," I said.

"Really?" She looked up and smiled.

"Sure. You're smart, you know a lot of people, and you're up on where to go for what events. You'd be a natural."

"Thanks." Gloria grabbed my hand and squeezed. Then, as if she realized she'd over-stepped, she pulled her hand back. The smile remained, however.

"Besides," I said, "if you wear the same dress, men will donate like crazy."

"You just want to get me out of it later." I

nodded. Gloria grinned anew. "Make sure it gets folded neatly on the floor."

* * *

IT DIDN'T. Clothing ended up on the stairway in Gloria's house. So did we for a while. Gloria's steps are covered in soft carpeting, but her bed proved a lot more comfortable. Despite living alone, Gloria owned a king bed. Our lustful romps took us over every centimeter of it at some point or another. When we had worn ourselves out, we both collapsed near the middle.

In the morning, I padded downstairs while Gloria slept. This made only the second time I'd seen her eat-in kitchen. I wanted one transplanted directly into my apartment. The problem was her kitchen would have consumed most of my place. For all the square footage, Gloria did very little cooking and confessed her efforts rarely ended well. I rummaged around until I found a skillet and some cooking utensils. The paucity of the refrigerator contents would have embarrassed many a bachelor—me included—but I could work with it. I found a half-dozen eggs, some butter, spinach, and a cheese that sounded fancy—and bore an expensive price tag—but smelled exactly like provolone.

Fifteen minutes later, I set two spinach and cheese omelets on the kitchen table, along with toast from a French baguette, and two steaming mugs of coffee. True to form, Gloria came downstairs a minute later. Eggs and coffee got her every time. "Wow," she said as she sat, "thanks for making breakfast."

"Thanks for having a great kitchen," I said.

"You do pretty well in yours." Gloria ate a bite of her omelet and nodded in appreciation.

"I could do a lot better here, especially if you stocked the fridge."

"Stay over more often, then," Gloria said with a smile. I smiled, too. Then, as if we both realized what our words meant, we ate and drank coffee in silence for a few minutes.

After we finished the omelets and toast and I poured us each a second cup, Gloria said, "Did you get what you needed last night?"

"For quite a while, yes," I said, grinning.

Color rose in Gloria's cheeks. "I meant from the fundraiser."

"I'll look in a little while," I said.

"Not in a rush?"

I shrugged. "If Father Larry is involved, waiting until I get home won't change anything. If he's not, he has to know who it is, and I'll still be able to get the info from his phone."

"What if he deletes the contact and texts?"

"Nothing really gets deleted," I said. "Most stuff is easy to recover."

Gloria stood and sashayed a few steps to me. "Since you're not in a hurry . . ." She swung a shapely leg over me and lowered herself onto my lap. "I got what I needed last night, too," she breathed into my ear. I felt the hairs on my arms stand at attention. "But I think I need more." She planted an aggressive kiss on me.

"I think I do, too," I said.

* * *

BACK IN MY OFFICE, I connected my phone to my computer to comb through the results on a larger screen. Father Larry kept a lot of contacts, none with any context. Because he was a priest, I presumed the women were parishioners or donors. maybe even friends, but not paramours. I saw a few names I recognized while skimming the list, but none jumped out at me.

I dumped Father Larry's phone calls into a database, then did the same for his texts. I could read them later; for now, I wanted to know who he called and texted the most. By a healthy margin, Father Larry's most frequent texting partner appeared in his contacts only as "D.V." The only two phone calls with this person both occurred more than a week before Dave Waugh's murder. I also checked Father Larry's voicemails. He deleted one from DV. The timestamp showed it came in shortly after the murder. I couldn't play the audio, but phone carriers transcribe voicemails now—helpful both for customers and the hackers who have jacked their data.

I heard it's done. He won't be a problem anymore.

Whoever D.V. was, he left a careful message. He "heard" whatever it is, so he didn't directly implicate himself. The "he" was never mentioned, and I imagined a good defense attorney crafting many flights of fancy wherein "he won't be a problem anymore" turned out as a benefit for the subject. The timing was convenient, easily spun as coincidental, and thus fell far short of being a smoking gun. Still, it gave me something to work with, a thread I could try to unravel.

To do so, I needed to find out who D.V. was. Father Larry wouldn't tell me. My gut said he would be as rude to me as a priest could be without feeling the soles of his shoes getting hot. A few clever Google searches later, associating D.V. with fundraising and St. Mark's, I uncovered Demetrius Vasilios. Another search told me he was the owner and proprietor of Vasilios Construction. An article in The Catholic Review mentioned his philanthropy and his formation of a committee to determine the company best suited to build the new St. Mark's. After exhaustive digging, Vasilios reached the shocking conclusion his company would be best. Several articles mentioned him as a generous donor to various Catholic charities and to St. Mark's in particular. None of them mentioned why.

With Google failing me, I went to conduct an offline search.

* * *

"What do you want to know about that greaser for?" Tony Rizzo said from across his table.

While much of Little Italy had gone upscale, Tony remained the same. He didn't alter his menu to accommodate changing tastes and desires for healthier food, and he could always be counted on for an ethnic slur. "Not a fan?" I said.

Tony waved his hand and scowled. "He's OK, I guess. Don't know why he likes the Catholics, though. Fucking Greeks have their own church."

"Maybe he's a fan of the First Amendment," I suggested.

My remark drew a snort from Tony. "My guess is he prefers the second."

Now we were getting somewhere. "So he's the type who might employ a goon or two." One of Tony's bruisers looked at me. "No offense." He did not look offended; in fact, his neutral expression made me wonder if he were alive.

"Definitely," Tony said.

I sipped my iced tea. When I came in, Tony offered me a meal as usual. I didn't want to make this a long visit, however. While I liked Tony, I knew my career choice didn't enthuse him, and I didn't want to lean on him for dirt on other people. "How legit is the construction business?" I said.

"Totally legit," said Tony. "It's a good company. They know how to get things done and how shit works."

His favorable review meant Tony had a piece of the company. Even the things he did as an organized crime boss were old school. He refused to dip his toe into the ransomware waters, for instance. If I mentioned it, I'm sure he would have a crack about the Russians at the ready. "He headed up some committee to find the best company to build the new St. Mark's," I said. "Guess which company he picked."

"His own. I know."

"You do?"

"You think a big construction project happens in Baltimore without me knowing about it?"

"I suppose not." I waited. Tony hadn't been this specific during our recent conversation.

"I didn't tell you everything I know before," he said. "No point dragging the wrong guy through the mud."

"Now we know he's dirty."

"Vasilios had the paperwork filed weeks ago. Had his permits lined up and everything."

"All before before the story hit," I said, "and before Dave Waugh was killed."

Tony frowned. "He the kid got stabbed near the church?"

"Yes."

"You think Vasilios did it?" I told Tony—without revealing my methods—what I learned about Vasilios' voicemail and texts with Father Larry. "Shitty court case," he said, "but you and I both know what happened."

I needed to ask this question. "Tony, would it hurt you if Vasilios went down for this?"

Tony smiled. I've known him most of my life, and I've seen him smile a lot. This one was sincere. "I appreciate you asking me," he said. "Vasilios has a younger brother, helps him with the company. Let's just say the kid brother knows how the game is played, too."

"All right," I said with a nod. "I don't know where this is going to go, but Vasilios looks dirty."

"He does." Tony looked at me for a moment. It started to get uncomfortable. "This is an interesting job for you, C.T. I feel your parents' influence in some of it. You're a smart kid. You know a lot of things. I think you can do good work for people."

"Thanks, Tony," I said.

"Don't mention it. Be sure to have a meal next

time you're here. You're my friend. I enjoy it when my friends eat here."

"I will." I'd try to stay on Tony's good side along the way. He stabled more muscle than Vasilios, and he hired from a better talent pool. I didn't need to end up on the wrong side of his ledger.

CHAPTER 8

Back at home, I researched Vasilios' company. Everything looked on the up-and-up. The company worked projects all across the state, turned a profit, paid bonuses to employees, and volunteered time and labor to charities. I found plenty of pictures of Vasilios smiling or shaking hands with someone else, usually a city or state luminary. More digging on local forums, blogs, Facebook posts, tweets, and subreddits revealed a few people displeased with Vasilios' success. They came armed with uncharitable theories. I figured those naysayers worked for construction companies which declined to pay Tony Rizzo. Vasilios paid his share, and one of the perks appeared to be a wealth of contracts in the city.

I thought about what Tony said. Dave Waugh going public, or the press turning his blog posts into a big story, would expose Father Larry's past and scuttle the new St. Mark's. Such an event would cost Vasilios in both money and reputation. I couldn't help but wonder if he greased any palms inside city hall. It would be more money down the drain or one or more angry city employees who wouldn't be getting the usual graft and could threaten future projects. Either way, bad for Vasilios.

The information was good, but I wanted more. I wanted dirt from inside the company. Their website looked like a professional designed it: it featured sharp pictures, a defined menu structure, and well-edited text. Like many sites, it ran on WordPress. WP is quite good, but as with any popular software or platform, people less ethical than I will discover and post its vulnerabilities. Then the company releases a patch, the hackers poke and prod the new version to discover the weaknesses, and so on. Such is the cycle of life for large software companies.

I soon discovered I didn't need a WordPress vulnerability, though. Vasilios' site had one far older. Database admins use a language called SQL to query and maintain their information stores. Users interact with them, on a basic level, via things like online forms. The databases are supposed to be protected from user malfeasance. However, some sites are vulnerable to people like me entering specific commands into a form and thus swiping the keys to the kingdom. SQL injection attacks have been known for years, and there are several methods to mitigate their effectiveness. Vasilios didn't use any of them. I got full access with a few dozen keystrokes.

It gave me a wealth of information: detailed employee records, accounts payable, accounts received, construction equipment, insurance policies, and a full listing of IT assets and accounts. Never one to refuse so obvious an invitation, I set my sights on a conference room PC. For some reason, it still ran Windows XP years after Microsoft ended support for the operating system. Once I got past the firewall, knocking over the XP box would be easy. I took my time and setup a connection to the conference room PC. One malicious payload later, and I took control of it.

Firewalls are good at keeping people out. Once you get in, however, most firewalls can do little to stop you. It's like a huge stone fence topped with razor wire. Getting past it is a challenge, but anyone who does no longer has to deal with the wall. I was on the inside now. Using the list of IT accounts, I made myself an administrator, migrated to a random server, and then pivoted to the email server. I didn't want to lose time reading the emails. The longer I lingered in the network, the higher the chance someone or something would take note of me. I downloaded email records from the important people in the company, erased my footprints, and logged off.

Something nagged at me, so I went back to the website. On the "Contact Us" page, I saw a link to email the administrator with any problems. I held my mouse over the link. It read *yanni@vasiliosconstr.biz*. Son of a bitch. Vasilios' son planted the confession idea in Ernie's head. I wondered how much he knew about the sins of his father. The old man needed to go down for this.

Light reading lay ahead to make it happen.

* * *

AFTER DOING some of the work onscreen, I needed a break for lunch. I also formulated an angle for what to do with my treasure trove of Vasilios' insider information. My plan required a little help, so I made a phone call and arranged to meet a friend for lunch.

Isabella's Brick Oven sat nestled among a bunch of other Italian *ristoranti* in Little Italy. It boasted of the best pizza of all of them, however, so when Joey Trovato suggested it, I jumped at the prospect. The beige brickwork and classic green awning hearkened back to a different era of restaurants, before things like tasting menus and gluten-free crusts. Perhaps feeling a bit regal, I ordered the

King Richard with four different kinds of meat, then sat at a booth across from Joey.

Joey was a black Sicilian who'd struggled with his weight since we were kids. Despite being six feet tall and three hundred pounds, Joey possessed a surprising amount of athleticism. I knew a bunch of skinny people who couldn't outrun him in a distance race. None of them could keep up with him at a dinner table, either. When I saw Joey nursing a soda and a small eggplant parmesan sub, I was surprised. He most likely expected a pizza and something else still coming out.

"Hi, C.T. Been a couple weeks."

"I can't afford to take you to lunch every week," I said.

Joey grinned. "Sure you can."

"We could meet at your house. I know you can cook."

"I ain't providing the expertise *and* the meal," said Joey.

"Who said this wasn't a social call?"

"You did."

"Right," I said. "Fair enough." The waitress dropped off my pizza. It looked like a meal baked for royalty. The meat generously added, the cheese perfectly golden brown, and the crust managed to look both light and substantial at the same time. There are few substitutes for a good brick-oven pie.

I let it cool for a minute before separating a piece and taking a bite. Delicious.

"Where's your pizza?" I said before taking another bite.

"Eh. I'm not very hungry."

I'm rarely struck speechless, but Joey admitting to not being hungry did it. All I could manage between my surprise and mouthfuls was a confused, "Mmm?"

"I had an early lunch," Joey said. "It followed an early breakfast and a mid-morning brunch."

"Makes sense to have a small fourth meal, then," I said. "Gotta save room for the fifth and sixth."

"You're hilarious."

I ate more pizza while Joey finished his sub. After a few minutes, he said, "So what can I do for you today?"

"You've heard of Vasilios Construction?"

"Most people have."

"Most people don't know the owner might be a killer," I whispered.

"Seriously?" he said. I nodded. "Damn. What can I do?"

Joey, like me, worked to help people. He set them up with new identities. He'd been doing it for at least five years. Anytime I needed information about someone who might have disappeared, I talked to Joey. He's seen a lot of people, heard their bad beat stories, and helped them vanish. I could have asked him about Dave Waugh, but I had something else in mind. "Can you make me a press ID?" I said.

Joey frowned. "Being a crusading detective ain't enough?"

"It's more than enough." I paused. "I just . . . have an angle on this one. I think a press ID would allow me to play it up."

"I'm sure you could make one yourself."

"But not a good one. Not one to stand up to scrutiny." A little flattery never hurt. Besides, Joey did excellent work.

"OK," Joey said. "Text me a good picture of yourself."

"Could take a while," I said. "There are so many to choose from."

"I know the feeling," Joey said with a smile.

"Can you drop it off later?"

"You trying to rush greatness?"

I put my hand over my chest and feigned offense. "Me? Never. I am, however, trying to keep greatness on a reasonable schedule."

"Fine," Joey said. "I'll drop it by later."

"Thanks," I said. "It'll give me time to do some more light reading."

"Do I want to know?"

"Probably not."

"Will it help you bust Vasilios?"

"It's my hope."

Joey raised his mostly-empty glass. "To freedom of the press," he said.

* * *

JOEY DELIVERED my press ID a couple hours later. The handsome face looking at me through the plastic belonged to Trent Reasoner of The Investigative Voice. "Is this paper still a thing?" I said.

"Last I checked," said Joey.

I thought about objecting to the name, realized I had no ground to stand on, and scuttled the idea. Joey left, and I finished my research. I read a bunch of internal emails where Vasilios made reference to St. Marks, plus a few veiled mentions of Tony Rizzo. Any references to Dave Waugh were framed by the problems a murder would present to the new St. Mark's project. One email written the morning after Dave Waugh's murder celebrated the fact an unnamed individual got what was coming to him. No further context. It didn't constitute a smoking gun, a cooling gun, or a gun of any sort. I was trying to hit a bull's eye twenty-five yards down range with a hammer.

Getting back into Vasilios' network could give me more ammo. People have gotten more careful in email over the years as accounts get compromised and legitimate records get subpoenaed. Maybe

Vasilios harbored something incriminating on his personal shared drive. It wasn't likely, though. Any administrator could have accessed it, and I doubted Vasilios wanted the IT staff to know he took delight in someone's murder. Those things caused people to ask questions.

I looked at my watch. If Vasilios was as hard-working as his website wanted me to believe, he would still be at the office.

Armed with my press credential—and a pistol in the car—I drove to Vasilios Construction.

* * *

THE CLOCK STRUCK four o'clock as I pulled into the parking lot. Vasilios Construction sat in an industrial area of Baltimore on Holabird Avenue. Some of the industry here left when GM shuttered their nearby plant on Broening Highway in 2005. Then a few years ago, Amazon took over the space and used it as a distribution center. It was another sign of the old economy changing in Baltimore. Once-thriving buildings were either razed or remained as decaying ghosts of the bygone era. Soon, only the port would be left. I had no idea if the Amazon facility counted as industry, but I enjoyed getting my packages four hours after I ordered them.

A one-story building about the size of a large

rancher looked like the company's office. Past it were a bunch of garages and other spots to keep heavy equipment. I watched someone park a backhoe as easily as I parked my Lexus before I walked into the office. The secretary managed to give me a look merging friendly and wary. She might broadcast a good smile if she cared to. Maybe they weren't used to handsome men walking through the door here. "Can I help you?" I guessed the woman for late thirties. Curly blonde hair framed glasses, and she wore a blue company polo. The friendliness faded from her expression.

I showed her my press credential. "I'd like to ask Mr. Vasilios some questions."

She studied the ID through chic narrow lenses. "Mr. Reasoner?" I nodded. "Did you make an appointment?"

"I'm afraid not," I said, giving her a high-wattage smile. I didn't offer my best smile, merely a good one. Vasilios didn't need his secretary fawning over me, after all.

"What's the nature of your visit?" she said.

"Someone showed me some . . . documents which don't paint the company in a good light. I haven't released them. I was hoping to talk to Mr. Vasilios about them."

"I'll see if he can fit you in." She stood and walked away. Two doors were behind her desk, making her a semi-literal gatekeeper. She opened the one on the left and disappeared down a hall-way. I sat on a padded blue task chair of moderate comfort. The secretary's desk held two computers and three monitors, plus a bunch of notebooks, calendars, and schedules. Vasilios needed some apps. Other calendars hung on the walls nearby, each marked up in different colors. Blue dominated the office from the chairs to the window trim to the mood.

A minute later, the lady returned with two men who were not Vasilios. One was the spiky-haired blond goon I met before. The other one was of similar size and build and probably employed for the same reason. "Mr. Vasilios can't see you right now," she said, struggling to contain a grin. "These gentlemen will talk to you instead. Outside." I took this to mean Vasilios' secretary knew he was dirty. She reveled in it. I expected her to watch from the window while Tweedleblond and Tweedledumb tried to convince me to stay away.

"Yeah, outside," the blond one aped her sarcastic tone. His partner wore his brown hair in a short buzz and smiled like a fool.

"I guess we can do the interview outside," I said, playing along. I exited first, careful to keep an eye out for the legbreakers following me.

"You ain't no reporter," the other one said.

"And you're not an English teacher," I said as I walked toward my car parked about halfway down the lot. I watched my escorts in the reflections of every side window and windshield I passed.

"Keep walking, jerk," said the blond one.

About twenty paces later, I stopped at a vehicle not my own. My Lexus sat three spaces away. If we were going to fight, I didn't want my car to be collateral damage. I've owned it since my sophomore year of college, and Lexus doesn't make sports sedans with manual transmissions anymore. "Sure your boss doesn't want to talk to me?" I said.

The brown-haired one glared. "He told us to get rid of you." I didn't doubt it. I also didn't want to wait for his enforcers to make their moves. In the confines of a parking lot, I didn't want to have them dictate the situation to me. When Brown Buzz reached for me from my right, I gave him a quick, sharp jab to the solar plexus. It wouldn't put him down, but it would leave him sucking wind for a few seconds.

I immediately turned to my left. Spiky Hair processed what happened. Before the hamster spun the wheel fast enough for him to make a decision, I stomped on his foot. Pain made him bend down a little, where I elbowed him twice in the face, then shoved him headfirst into the closest car door. Brown Hair had recovered enough to glower and walk toward me by this point. I blocked his punch, slugged him in the stomach, and pulled his jacket over his head. While he flailed about, I boxed his ears, gave him two more good body shots, and put him down with a knee to the face.

I looked at the office. Sure enough, the secretary watched from the window. She didn't look happy. I waved to her as I walked to my car.

CHAPTER 9

AFTER I LEFT VASILIOS CONSTRUCTION, I drove to St. Mark's. Father Larry sat in his office reading a book. He frowned at me when he looked up. "'Hot tempers cause arguments, but patience brings peace,'" I said.

The glower softened. "Proverbs."

"It seemed appropriate."

"Did you Google it on the way over?" said Father Larry.

"Where's your faith in other people, Father?" I pointed at a guest chair. Father Larry sighed and nodded. "Considering the company you keep," I said, "I guess I shouldn't be surprised."

"What's that supposed to mean?" Father Larry closed his book, leaving the back facing up. I couldn't tell what it was.

"Your buddy Vasilios."

My comment made the priest frown anew, and

he paired it with a vigorous shake of his head. "No," he said. "Not Mr. Vasilios."

"He's in bed with the mob," I said. "He has professional goons on his payroll. And he has motive for wanting Dave Waugh dead."

"That's ridiculous."

"Father, the only two people a preponderance of evidence shows would have wanted to kill Dave are you and Vasilios." I paused while Father Larry continued to wag his head. "I'm pretty sure you didn't do it. Process of elimination leaves your benefactor."

"Perhaps it was a robbery." Father Larry said.

"Not many robbers stab their victims a dozen times in the chest. It's barbarism and suggests hatred."

"What about—"

"He did it, or he ordered one of his men to do it." I watched Father Larry for a reaction. "I think you know it . . . or at least suspect."

Father Larry bowed his head and rubbed the bridge of his nose. "What do you want, Mr. Ferguson?"

"What I've always wanted: the truth."

"I'm tempted to tell you you couldn't handle it," he said with a small smile.

I grinned. "I appreciate the movie reference, Father, but I can take it."

"Fine." Father Larry looked around the room. I

followed his gaze as he looked at two Bibles and a crucifix. Maybe they gave him the inspiration he sought. "I'd suspected for a while that Mr. Vasilios knew more than he told me."

"You two talked about Dave Waugh's murder?" I said.

"He was our major benefactor. It's hard to avoid telling someone like him that a man was murdered almost on our doorstep."

"Fair enough."

"Anyway, Mr. Vasilios didn't seem very surprised, even though he said he hadn't heard. He told me all the right things."

"Why not go to the police?"

"With what?" the priest said. "I had a suspicion. That's all."

"And he's building you a new church," I said.

Father Larry paused, then nodded. "Yes. I admit that shouldn't have been a consideration, but I wanted the best for our congregation."

"So you never clued in the cops?"

"Only the basics," he said.

I started to say something, then stopped. Father Larry had come upon the murder scene. He would have seen it all. He hadn't told the police anything special. "You're Ernie Chin's source," I said. "The one he wouldn't give up."

"Yes," Father Larry said with a nod. "I've known

Ernie for a couple years. I admit his blog is ghoulish, but he does good work."

"But the things you told him, the level of detail?"

"I have two brothers in law enforcement. Heard a lot of shop talk."

"What were you hoping to accomplish?" I said.

"I meant what I said about wanting the best for our congregation. There was another part of me, though, that wanted to see justice done. I didn't know if Mr. Vasilios had done anything, but I felt he knew more than he should have. I hoped the police would look into it."

"Why not simply tell them?"

Father Larry smiled. It didn't reach his eyes. "Mr. Vasilios usually talks to me in the confessional."

"Clever," I said. "He figures you won't break the sacrament."

"I haven't. I can't."

"What about the conversation we're having right now?"

"You know a lot already." Father Larry shrugged. "I haven't mentioned anything he told me in confidence."

An organ played in the background as I pondered how to get Father Larry to dime out his money man. Even in the rectory, the speakers carried the sound well enough for me to recognize the song. "*Ave Maria*," I said.

"Our organist practices on Friday evenings," Father Larry said, "not that she needs it."

An idea wormed its way into my brain. If I couldn't get Father Larry to give up Vasilios, maybe I could induce Vasilios to give himself up unwittingly.

"Father, does Vasilios take confession regularly?"

"He does, every Saturday before the five o'clock service. He comes in around four-fifteen."

"So you expect to see him tomorrow?" I said.

"Yes."

"Do you think you could get him to confess?"

Father Larry recoiled. "It's a sacrament, not an interrogation."

"You obviously get along with him," I said. "He trusts you. He wants to build a new church with you at the center. Do you think you could steer the conversation toward a real confession?"

"Even if I could," Father Larry said, "I don't see how that would help you. I won't break the sanctity of the confessional."

"I don't think I need you to, Father."

"I'm not sure I like the sound of that."

"The less you know, the better. But I have an idea. If you want to see justice done, it might work."

The priest sighed and sagged back in his chair. "And what do I have to do?"

"Nothing," I said.

"Nothing?"

"I'll take care of everything."

"I'm not sure I like this," Father Larry said.

"You won't be breaking any of your vows to the church," I said. "The Vatican isn't going to send someone to excommunicate you."

Father Larry considered it for a moment. "Very well," he said. "I will say this, Mr. Ferguson—if whatever you're planning goes south on you, I'm not going to give you any cover."

"Of course not, Father," I said. "Lying is a sin."

* * *

I CALLED Rich from my car. "What are you doing tonight?" I said when he answered.

"I just left the precinct," he said. "Haven't thought much about it. Why?"

"Would you still describe yourself as an audiophile?"

"Have you seen my stereo?"

"No one has stereos anymore."

"My point." Rich paused. "Wait, what plan are you thinking up involving my system?"

"Nothing," I said. "Your stereo will not be harmed in the execution of my scheme."

"Good thing," said Rich.

"I do, however, need your knowledge of wiring and sound."

"For what? Is this about the blogger?"

"I'll be by your house in an hour," I said.

"Can't wait," Rich said and hung up.

He needed to wait about an hour and five minutes. Rich lived in Hamilton in a large Victorian he bought when his parents, my aunt and uncle, died. I loved the large yard and detached garage. Rich's house could have fit my apartment inside it at least three times over. The structure must have been a century old, and it showed its age in a few areas. Rich, however, modernized it with his own two hands—new windows, new paint, a better porch, and wood flooring. Plus other fixes I hadn't seen. If he hadn't chosen the Army and police route, my cousin could have been a hell of a carpenter.

Rich offered me a beer when I walked in. It was an IPA, so I accepted. For his part, Rich drank some pale wheat beer. "What's this about?" he said when we had each lubricated our throats.

"I think I know who killed Dave Waugh," I said.

"You think?"

We sat on opposite ends of the large sofa in Rich's living room. I laid it all on the table for him. He nodded a few times during my monologue but never interrupted. "The priest won't break the confessional. I had an idea to make his stubbornness irrelevant."

"And it involves wiring something for audio?" Rich said.

"Yes."

"What?"

"The confessional," I said.

"Are you crazy?" said Rich. "You can't wire a confessional for sound."

"Why not?"

"Because it's . . . it's wrong."

"It's a small, enclosed room," I said. "It's not far from two large speakers. Hypothetically, if the priest got Vasilios to confess and everyone heard it, we'd have him."

"I wish I were a lawyer," Rich said. "This doesn't sound like it will hold up."

"Why not? He's not confessing under duress."

Rich took a long swig of his beer. As weak as it looked, he would need a couple more bottles to come around. "There's a reasonable expectation of privacy in a confessional," he said.

"Now you sound like a lawyer," I said.

"Someone like Vasilios is going to have good lawyers."

"Then use his public confession to go after him," I said. "Even things like his company emails."

"Why his company emails?" Rich narrowed his eyes at me. "What did you do?"

"Nothing. I happen to think someone like Vasilios might drop hints in an email."

"Incredible," Rich said, shaking his head. "If you've read the guy's emails, why go to all this trouble?"

"If I did something like you're hinting, the police would still need to do it legally as part of the investigation."

Rich finished his beer in one pull and rolled his eyes. He left the room and came back a moment later with a second bottle. I looked at the stereo dominating the massive entertainment center. Rich accrued the pieces over the years and wired everything together himself, including the seven speakers. The size of the system made it the focus of Rich's spartan living room, not the more modest TV. "What about sound in the confessional?" Rich said.

"What do you mean?"

"If we wire it for audio, they'll be able to hear everything in there, too. Vasilios will know he's being broadcast."

"Shit," I said. "Is there a way to silence it?"

"Short of fully soundproofing it, no." Rich paused. "But we might be able to mitigate it."

"Good."

"What's our time frame?"

"We have to start tonight and finish by morning."

"Jesus Christ," Rich said, shaking his head. "You really think this could work?"

"You think you can do the wiring?" I said.

"Yes."

"Then I'll say yes, too. I think it could work."

"I need to get a few things together," Rich said. He looked at his beer. "And I might need another of these. Give me about fifteen minutes."

"Take your time," I said.

At the specified time, Rich came back into the room carrying a box and a duffel bag. "Let's go before I change my mind," he said.

So we went.

* * *

FIVE HOURS LATER, we finished. Getting into the church had been easy. Places designed to welcome people rarely invest in good locks. Rich and I called an audible after we got there. The confessional is near the back of the church, so we wired it into the speakers only at the front of the church. I brought two small microphones and a speaker I previously bought from the local spy store. We set up the mikes to broadcast to the front and spliced off a speaker wire into the well-hidden small one. The organ music it would pipe into the confessional should eliminate the odds of Vasilios overhearing himself telling everything to Father Larry. The combination of a small speaker and a low volume setting would prevent the rerouted music from being too loud.

If the priest upheld his part of the deal.

I couldn't worry about those details at two-thirty in the morning, however. The good father knew his role in this. He said he could do it, and on some level, I think he wanted justice for Dave Waugh. Now I needed him to come through. If he didn't, I would need to dig deeper into the network at Vasilios Construction and hope for the best.

I settled into a fitful sleep.

* * *

By four o'clock, I was in St. Mark's and told Father Larry of our plan. Without acknowledgement, he helped by having the sacristan rope off the first three pews. Rich was already there along with two officers I recognized only after picturing them in uniform. I sat in the second pew, right in front of Rich. When Vasilios came in, I hoped Rich's body would screen me from his view. While I sat there, I tried to look devout. It was a struggle.

"I didn't expect the pews to be roped off," Rich whispered.

"Good move," I said, keeping my voice low.

"I'm not so sure. People are going to wonder why we're sitting here."

"Wonder, sure. They're not going to come up and ask us about it. No one wants to make a scene like that in church."

"I hope you're right," said Rich.

"I am."

To keep myself from turning to look for Vasilios, I tried to focus on the organ. Even with the speaker rewiring Rich and I had done, the music came through at what sounded like normal volume. I wondered if we would strain to hear Vasilios' confession.

About ten minutes crawled by, and Rich said, "He's here." I half-turned and saw Vasilios walk in, accompanied by one of the goons who had chased me back to my apartment. Neither appeared to notice me, but I turned around and slouched in the pew in case.

"I hope they didn't see me," I said.

"Doesn't look like it," Rich said, shaking his head. "He's chatting with the priest now. The other guy is sitting in the last row." Rich paused. I waited. "It looks like Toohey waved to the organist. Now they went in."

The organ music grew softer and featured more high notes. Voices came through the speakers. "Good to see you again," Father Larry said.

"Always good to be here," said Vasilios.

"Shall we begin?" If Father Larry were nervous, I couldn't hear it in his voice.

"Bless me, Father, for I have sinned. It's been a week since my last confession."

"Anything you'd like to talk about?" Father Larry sounded like a shrink. I hoped he stopped before asking Vasilios how killing Dave Waugh made him feel.

"The usual," Vasilios said. "It's hard to run a successful business without being a sinner."

Chatter went up in the church, meaning others noticed the voices coming through the speakers. We didn't need them to interfere. Rich and I added some soundproofing to the confessional, but it wasn't complete or foolproof. Some idiot yelling at or banging on the door would spoil everything.

"It's under control," Rich said.

"What do you mean?" I said.

"We have officers over there. No one will interrupt them."

"We'd better hope the bodyguard isn't given to shouting, then."

". . . angered Jesus," we heard Father Larry say.

"Wasn't that about gambling?" Vasilios said. "I don't gamble. Well, not in the traditional sense." Sure. He just murdered people or ordered someone in his stable of hired muscle to do it.

Father Larry's sigh came through the speakers

as a soft hiss. "Mr. Vasilios, I think there's something else. Something . . . below the surface."

"What are you, my shrink now?" Valid question. The priest would need to walk a tightrope here.

"Not at all," Father Larry said. "But I can see it in your face. I hear it in your voice. God sees it in your heart."

"You mean that kid?" Vasilios said.

"What kid?"

"You know, the prick with the blog."

"This is a church," Father Larry said.

"Sorry, Father. The guy who was writing all the sh . . . all the stuff. He kicked up a lot of dirt. We couldn't have it."

"Should we seek forgiveness through prayers to cleanse your soul?"

"I never told you this. Good thing we're in the confessional." Vasilios paused, took a deep breath, and kept going. " The blog guy guy was a problem. If his story got picked up, it could have ruined everything."

"A new St. Mark's could have another priest," said Father Larry.

"Not the same church, then," Vasilios said. "We don't want someone else. We need you, Father. You're flawed like we are. When you preach about mistakes and regret, I can feel it. It's real. Other priests don't know anything about that."

"I'm flattered, Demetrius, but what are you saying?"

"The guy needed to die. So I had Johnny do it."

Rich nodded, and a smile spread across his face. "We got him," he said. "It worked."

I looked around the church. We weren't the only ones interested in the conversation coming from the confessional. The rest of the congregation surged to one side of the church. If they rushed the door, three cops wouldn't keep them at bay. Even the goon in the back row moved up. When he started toward the confessional, one of the cops interceded and kept him back.

"Let's go," Rich said. He and the two other officers stood, and I went with them to the other side of the church. Rich's badge cleared a path for us. Vasilios' bodyguard spotted me and glowered. I smiled at him and waved, which did not improve his mood. When Rich pounded on the confessional door, the henchman tried to slip away. Two cops stopped him and encouraged him to take a seat.

Father Larry opened the door. Vasilios sat in a small chair. He frowned at everyone. "What's the meaning of this interruption?" Father Larry said.

"Demetrius Vasilios, you're under arrest," Rich said.

The congregation applauded while Rich Mirandized Vasilios, interrupted several times by the latter's crowing about his attorneys. The two cops who came with Rich led Vasilios away, and the other three escorted his sidekick.

"I hope we can make this stick," I said.

"Me, too," said Rich. "Hey, at least now you can give Liz Fleming some good news."

Maybe she'd even be wearing a short skirt this time.

CHAPTER 10

THE NEXT MORNING, MY CELL PHONE BUZZING on the nightstand woke me. I glanced at the clock as I answered: seven forty-five. Ugh.

"We're going to question Vasilios soon," Rich said. "I figured you might want to sit in."

"Wow, thanks," I said. "You sure a mere civilian like me can hang with a detective like you?"

"Try to keep up," Rich said, and then broke the call.

I showered quickly, then grabbed a breakfast sandwich and coffee at Dunkin' Donuts en route to the precinct. I almost indulged in a donut, but that would have made me feel too much like a cop. I didn't need the feeling anytime but especially not before nine AM. Inside the station, I found Rich at his desk and dropped off the extra coffee I bought for him. "A token of appreciation," I said.

"Thanks," said Rich before he took a sip. "You ready?"

"Do I get to ask questions?"

"Probably best if you keep them to a minimum."

"How's Vasilios still here, anyway?" I said. "Wealthy assholes like him should have lawyers who could spring them."

"We're still considering charges," Rich said, and a smile spread over his lips. "His mouthpiece's pissed and self-righteous, but there's nothing he can do about it."

"Sounds like it'll be fun," I said, and we went to the interview room. It was about ten by ten, with a large table and four shabby chairs in the center. A darkened window dominated the left wall. Vasilios sat in a chair on the far side, handcuffed to a bar on the tabletop. His expression resembled someone who sucked a lemon for an hour. His lawyer, a paunchy black man with a full head of gray hair, looked equally cheery.

"My client does not need to be shackled," the attorney said when Rich closed the door.

"He's not," Rich said. "He's just cuffed."

"You know what I meant."

"Sure, but you bastards always twist what other people say." Rich sat, took out a key, and undid Vasilios' cuffs. "How's it feel to be on the other end?"

The lawyer didn't take the bait. Instead, he nodded toward me and said, "Who's this?"

"The private investigator who figured out what happened," said Rich.

"A civilian?"

"You're a civilian," I pointed out.

"I'm an attorney at law," he said as if it were a point of pride.

"I was trying to be nice."

While the lawyer seethed, Rich said, "Mr. Johnstone, your client confessed to his role in the murder of Dave Waugh."

"I was set up," Vasilios said, rubbing his wrist. He pointed at me. "This prick must've had something to do with it."

I stayed quiet rather than give in to the barb. Later, I would need to pat myself on the back for this show of restraint. "A bunch of people at the church heard him," Rich said. " They make a lot of witnesses for the state's attorney."

"And just why was everyone able to hear my client's words?" Johnstone said. "Confession shouldn't be open mike night."

"Faulty wiring," Rich said.

"Faulty wiring?"

"There's little difference between a speaker and a microphone."

"We'll have some questions about that, I'm sure. Now, what are you charging my client with?"

Rich went over the list, which was voluminous, and Johnstone protested, which was pointless. "Take it up at the bail hearing," Rich said.

"We will," Johnstone said.

Rich and I left while Johnstone conferred with his slimy client. We got intercepted by Lieutenant Leon Sharpe emerging from the observation room. Sharpe was black, bald, and built like a defensive end. When he turned to face us, I saw the bars on his collar. He had been upgraded to captain.

"Captain," Rich said with a nod.

"Gentlemen," said Sharpe. He stopped in the middle of the hallway, blocking anyone over eighty pounds from squirting past him. "Good work on this one."

"Thanks," Rich and I said at the same time.

"Was the wiring really faulty?"

"I thought it was quite good," I said.

Sharpe smirked. "I'm gonna keep watching you," he said to me. Then he turned and walked the other direction.

"He just got promoted a couple weeks ago," Rich said when we were back at his desk.

"What does that mean for you?"

He shrugged. "Nothing yet. Sharpe oversees violent crime enforcement. He's in my command chain but not directly above me. Took him a while to get moved up." Rich lowered his voice. "A lot of people associate him with door-kicking and arresting."

"Aren't those good things?" I said.

"Depends who you talk to. Some say it got a little out of hand, went into harassment territory. Then you add in Freddie Gray and the DOJ report. Leon got some blowback there. But he's smart enough to adapt and overcome."

"Should I be concerned he's going to keep an eye on me?"

Rich grinned. "Probably."

* * *

SINCE I WAS ALREADY DOWNTOWN, I doubled down on the fun by stopping by the Public Defender's Office. To my surprise, I found Liz Fleming there on a Sunday. "You are a very dedicated public servant," I said as I poked my head in.

Sunday must have meant a relaxed dress code. I didn't mind. Standing at a shopworn file cabinet, Liz wore jeans hugging all the right places along with a sweater one size too small. She grinned. It didn't measure up to her smile, but I could live with it. "Just catching up on paperwork."

"How's Ernie?" I walked in and sat in one of her guest chairs. Their comfort had not improved.

"Free," Liz said. "He got released early this morning."

"Good. I hope he's learned something from all this."

"Me, too."

"I'll have to check his blog later," I said. "His lessons need to extend past traffic increases and monetization."

"If he does something like this again," Liz said, "he's on his own."

"Did you talk to him?"

Liz nodded. She pulled a large mug of coffee from behind her laptop. Now I wanted another cup. I was far too young to be up so early on a Sunday. "For a minute or so, right before he got out. He was very grateful to us."

"Us?" I said with a smile.

"Hey!" said Liz, "I filed some paperwork like a boss." She grinned again. Even though she co-opted some of the credit, I would work with her any time.

"I suppose you did. Good thing, too—I'm much better at fighting off goons than I am at busywork."

"We made a pretty good team," Liz said, more or less echoing my thoughts.

"Maybe next time, you can do more of the heavy lifting."

The remark got me a full smile. "But you do it so well. Sure you don't want a job?"

"I have a job," I said.

"Yes." Liz scrutinized me. I didn't give her a

reaction. Her inspection spilled over into checking-me-out territory. I didn't mind. "That's still a bit of a mystery."

"Maybe one of your investigators can solve it. If they're not too busy or too incompetent."

"We have good investigators," Liz said, frowning.

"And yet you worked with me," I said, "the newcomer with the mysterious background."

"They were busy."

"I'm sure they were."

Liz looked down at a file on her desk. "I need to get back to my work, Mr. Ferguson. Thanks for coming by." So much for any flirting. If I teamed with Liz again, I would have to stop before comparing myself to her investigators.

"Anytime." I stood. "And call me C.T."

"OK, C.T. Maybe I'll see you sometime."

I hoped so. "Maybe you will," I said and left Liz's office.

* * *

LATER IN THE DAY, the news told me Vasilios had been held over for trial. His motion for bail was denied. His lawyer, whose hair looked like it grayed a bit more since I saw him, told the press about Vasilios' strong business record, philanthropy, etc. None of it spared him from being an asshole, of course, and a killer on top of it all. The attorney also mentioned some rogue investigation. I felt a subpoena would be in my future, and I didn't relish the thought.

Around dinnertime, my cell phone rang with the call I expected. "Hi, Mom."

"Coningsby, your father and I saw the news," she said. My mother always called me by my full name, a family name on her side. I lived with it because pointing it out made her ramp up the frequency. "I'm glad you were able to help that poor young man."

"He really landed in the soup," my father said in the background.

"Tell Dad Ernie jumped into the soup," I said. "There may have been a nudge, but no one pushed him, and I needed to be talked into tossing him a life preserver."

"You can't pick and choose like that, Coningsby."

"Of course I can. I only have so much time. If you want me to help the people who really need it, I have to filter out the less needy ones."

My mother sniffed. She did so whenever someone said something to offend her sensibilities. Every time we spoke, she sniffed more than a cocaine addict craving a line and a mirror. It almost made up for her calling me by my full first name.

"Yes, well, make sure you're not turning away the people you really ought to help."

"Ernie ended up with the public defender," I said. "They didn't have any investigators to spare, so his lawyer asked me to help out. I'd already told him no."

"She must be a very pretty woman," my mother said in a mirthful tone.

She knew me too well. "I can neither confirm nor deny her pulchritude."

"Of course not, dear. I hope that awful man who did it gets what's coming to him."

"He's rich and has an expensive lawyer," I said. "We'll see."

"You're so cynical, Coningsby."

"Mom, if you missed the correlation between money and justice, I'm not sure I can help you at this point."

"Anyway," she said, tabling a side conversation I knew she didn't want to have, "your father and I will put ten thousand in your account tomorrow." This was the arrangement Liz didn't know about. Technically, I worked for my parents' charitable foundation. In reality, doing my job got me back into their good graces after my hacker friends and I got arrested in Hong Kong. After nineteen days in a Chinese prison, I would have agreed to almost any devil's bargain.

"Thanks, Mom."

"You take care, dear. Come by for dinner one night this week."

"I will."

"Maybe you can ask that lawyer to come with you," said my mother.

"Mom! I'm not bringing her for dinner."

"Very well, dear. Goodbye."

"Bye, Mom." We hung up. Down the hall, the business line in my office rang. It was Sunday. I had closed a case and money would be waiting for me tomorrow. No need to ruin the rest of the weekend by answering my phone. I let it go to voicemail. A new case could wait for the new work week.

THE END

Hi! Thanks for reading this novella. I hope you enjoyed reading it as much as I did writing it.

Here are the other books in my catalog:

The C.T. Ferguson Crime Novels:

1. The Reluctant Detective
2. The Unknown Devil
3. The Workers of Iniquity
4. Already Guilty
5. Daughters and Sons
6. A March from Innocence
7. Inside Cut
8. The Next Girl
9. In the Blood
10. Right as Rain
11. Dead Cat Bounce (December 2021)

The C.T. Ferguson Crime Novellas:

1. The Confessional (book 1.5 in overall series continuity)
2. Land of the Brave (2.5)
3. Red City Blues (3.5)
4. Blood on Canvas (8.5)

The John Tyler Action Thrillers

1. The Mechanic
2. White Lines
3. Lost Highway
4. Four on the Floor (Spring 2022)

While these are the suggested reading sequences, each novel is a standalone mystery or thriller, and the books can be enjoyed in whatever order you happen upon them.

Do you like free books? You can get the prequel novella to the C.T. Ferguson mystery series for free. *Hong Kong Dangerous* is unavailable for sale and is exclusive to my readers. Visit https://www.subscribepage.com/hkd2020 to get your book!

Connect with me: For the many ways of finding and reaching me online, please visit https://tomfowlerwrites.com/ contact. I'm always happy to talk to readers.

This is a work of fiction. Characters and places are either fictitious or used in a fictitious manner.

"Self-publishing" is something of a misnomer. This book would not have been possible without the contributions of many people.

- The great cover design team at 100 Covers.
- My editor extraordinaire, Chase Nottingham.
- My wonderful advance reader team, the Fell Street Irregulars.